MORE FROM
TONY DEL DEGAN

NOVELS and NOVELLAS

Sacrosanct
Rusthook
In River Cardinal
Ceres
The Recognition
The Plight of Steel

SHORT STORIES

The Chrysalis
Depthcrusher
Moist Gossamer
The Becoming
Eden Sank to Grief
Do Not Stand By My Grave, I Am Not There
The Bus from the Inner City
My Front Door, a Finchhole
Bolverkr

 Visit tony.deldegan.ca to explore the Red Runnel universe.

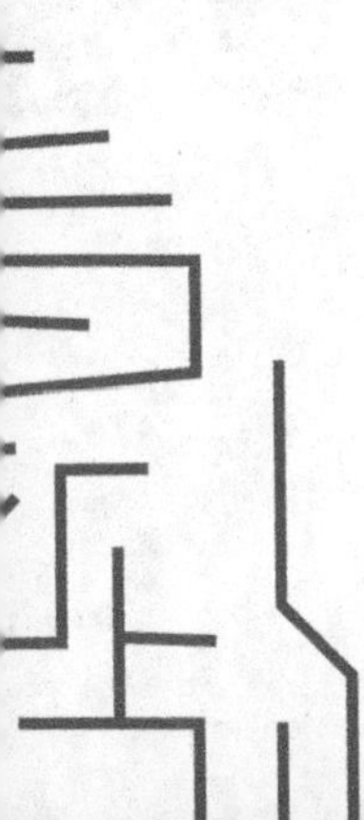

IN RIVER CARDINAL

BY TONY DEL DEGAN

tony.deldegan.ca

Second paperback edition 2026

For Dante and Leo.

THE TECHNICIAN

"A Dewbox bleeds when it receives a new file. Careful not to spill onto expensive equipment."

He took up the forceps, then tried to finger the handle of the screwdriver with his remaining digits. "Shit." His free hand took over–picked up the screwdriver. Flesh was peeled back by metal, and the Philip's head entered the wet. It slipped once or twice on moisture, but managed to free the screw. It popped out, fell into his hand, all red.

The driver pried the panel. It came out reluctantly. Now the internals were exposed. He found the wayward connection, soldered the wires, and reinserted the panel. No screw. It was gone–fallen off the table. He got down on his knees and scrounged about through the mess on the floor– papers, boxes, parts. His glasses were falling down–he nudged them back up the bridge of his nose.

"A Dewbox bleeds when it receives a new file. Careful not to spill onto expensive equipment."

He found it under a box. He plucked it with his fingers, then settled himself back onto his rolling stool. Smoke wisps grew from the glowing butt of a cigarette pinched in his grin. Though it protested, he worked the screwdriver until he felt the bite of metal threads. He released the forceps and sealed the flesh with tape.

"A Dewbox bleeds when it rec-"

Bang! "Shut up, fucking thing." Glowing ash settled in his beard and burned. He brushed it off. The cigarette was short; he spit it away and pulled a new one from his coat. He lit it and puffed, and looked down at the Dewbox through smoke. It was black, and textured like stingray. Tall as a child, with the voice of a woman. She could only speak two sentences. He tested it now, opening the receiver slot.

"A Dewbox bleeds when it receives a new file. Careful not to spill onto expensive equipment."

—

"Faulty connection. It should work now."

"Oh, thanks. Damn piece of shit, eh? No offense." He tugged on the lapel of his jacket. Off his desk came a file folder–red paper inside, with white writing. The slot *ka-chunked* open at the touch of his finger, and the metal teeth hung anxiously apart while the folder slid between. *Snap!* In the dank office, the box chirped helpfully.

"A Dewbox bleeds when it receiv…"

Crimson traced a pathway stained into the rayskin—one aged and endlessly remade. A small lip caught the discharge, filtered it back inside.

"What is that shit anyway?" He put his hand on the box, rested on it.

"Machine oil."

A pause. "Looks like blood."

The cigarette in the technician's mouth sparked and threw embers.

"I've got so many files. Thought I'd get backed up. Then I'd probably get a lashing from Mister Lang." There was a nameplate on his desk. *Taylor Brody*. Two white insignias were embroidered into his collar—cardinals.

"Yeah." The technician crammed tools back into his bag.

A frown. "Got a visit from the Redhoods yesterday. Scary bastards. Big guns on 'em too. What are those, by the way? You'd know, wouldn't you?"

"*Steyr AUG*'s."

"Did you use those back then?"

"No. Those are Austrian." He zipped up the bag.

"We're going out to the bar tonight. Are you coming?" He sniffled; cigarette smoke wafted past his face.

"No. Have to fix Polly's Dewbox."

"Well shit." He let go of the box. It stopped spewing. "Old crow. Probably dropped a stapler in the mouth." A pause. "Why do these keep breaking, Dewey?" He shoved a hand in his pocket, leaned back on his desk to await an answer. His nose twitched.

"'Cause people keep breaking them."

A smile. "Guess I shouldn't have asked."

The technician left.

———

She sat at the front counter—it was gray marble. A nail file flung particulate in small clouds. She turned as she heard him enter, whipping her thin, golden eyeglass chain. "Ah. Good." The voice was matronly—a croak. "There's the thing." One thin pointer digit extended from a gnarled claw.

"What's the problem, ma'am?"

"You tell me, Mister Becker."

The technician examined the box, ran his hands along the rayskin. He found the tape and peeled it off, then produced his forceps and screwdriver.

"Will I lose the files?"

"No ma'am. They're still inside."

"Good." She watched him work, absently grating her nails. "It has a woman's voice. Who's the woman?"

"My wife."

"You don't have one."

"No. I don't."

She looked down her nose at him. That was just the structure of her visage. One hand fussed with her mane of golden hair. "You could imagine she's inside the box–all the boxes."

No answer.

"But you do, don't you?"

"I don't catch your meaning, ma'am." He pulled the screw out–red and wet.

"Hm. It's adorable, if not a bit macabre."

"I don't know big words, ma'am."

She snorted. "Right. I'm sure you don't. Stupid is as stupid does, ain't that right Forrest?"

The driver slipped. "I've never seen that movie."

Her red lips cut a smile. "You're charming, Mister Becker. How about you ask me out for a cocktail."

"I don't drink."

"But you smoke."

"Those are different things." He cleared his throat–pushed up his glasses.

Polly tilted her head sideways. "I can't seem to figure you. Maybe you're sad and aloof, and maybe you're just simple." She checked her nails. The file attacked a flaw.

"When did she pass?"

The technician grunted, dropped the butt of his cigarette. He pushed dark hair out of his eyes, then refit the plate and screwed it back in. He taped the rayskin and stood briskly, collecting his things. "That's all."

"But you'll let me test it out first." She stood. There was a red folder on her desk, and she slid it between the metal teeth. *Snap!* Oil spilled from its hole, was collected in the receptacle. The Dewbox recited its warning. She noted, "Such a brilliant device. I wonder how it works."

The technician waited.

Polly's skin wrinkled around a frown. "Doctor Molina wants you. Don't tarry."

"Broken box?"

"That is your job, is it not, Mister Becker?" The office chair groaned under her weight. She picked up the nail file and scraped.

—

Doctor Osian Molina, M.D., D.V.M., Psy.D.

The frosted glass clicked beneath his knuckles. He adjusted the grip on his toolbag. From inside, he heard a muffled "Come!", and turned the handle.

The doctor sat at his desk behind a veil of smoke, dark

against mustard yellow wallpaper. Drooping palm fronds shielded him like a striped cat. A cigar shed tobacco ash across a varnished wooden desktop, and onto his black velvet lap. "Ah! Mister Becker. Come, come. Please, have a seat."

"I'd prefer to get working. Thank you, doctor."

He threw up his hands, pinching his cigar. "As you wish." His eyes tracked the technician across the office.

"What's the problem with it?" The Dewbox seemed operational. The technician touched the jaws and they opened, then shut.

"A Dewbox bleeds when it re…"

He turned to the doctor.

"Not broken." His tie was slightly undone. He typically wore his clothing like armor–buttoned and tied. "I asked you here for another reason, Mister Becker. Sit, if you would."

The technician crossed to the desk and sat across from the doctor. He put his toolbag down beside him. There was an itch under his collar; he tried to scratch it.

"Forgive my deception. I had Polly ask you to fix my box."

"No need to apologize, doctor."

"Good. Thank you." Above him, painted on the wall, was a large cardinal perched inside a red sun. It was hidden behind the fronds–pecking out. "I wished to discuss a bit about you. You are a valuable employee, and I have noted your devotion to your work, as well as your continued maintenance of our equipment here. Will you tell me a bit about yourself?"

"I… I like to tinker."

"Yes, I can see that." He leaned forward in his chair, stamped out his cigar.

"I don't know… I… was in Vietnam."

"A practical man, then."

"Is there a reason for this visit, doctor?"

"Yes."

Silence.

"Go on."

"I like whiskey after work."

"Do you abuse it?"

"No."

"Never? Have you thought about it?"

"No. Not once."

The doctor pulled a tin from his jacket pocket. Little blue mints rattled around inside. One was crushed between his teeth. "Tobacco." The cigar smoldered in its ashtray. "Do you know how to keep secrets, Mister Becker? Have you ever heard something told to you by a friend, which you knew was private, and told another soul what it was?"

"I don't know many people."

"Do you know many people in this building?"

"Only the people that own boxes."

"Is that a lie?"

"I can recite their names if you'd like."

Osian Molina tapped the table with his finger. Most of his hair was gone, but there was a comb on his desk. "Mister Lang hired you for your inventiveness."

"I assume so."

"What have you managed to do here since your hiring?"

"I…" The technician frowned. "I invented the Dewbox."

"And how helpful it is. What else?"

A pause. "I only maintain them."

"Now I seem to recall that Mister Lang revoked your workshop. That was kind of you to give it up so cordially. He is a strong-headed man, with grand ideas."

Someone walked by the door. In the fluorescent glow under the clearance, the feet cast gyrating shadows.

"Of course, doctor."

"Yes, of course. Of course." The doctor took the ashtray and dumped it into a bin under his desk. "But I am part owner of this company." He stood from his chair. "You maintain the box of Otis Lang."

Silence.

"He's my partner, Mister Becker. And I know the answer already. I only wished to test you. I would like you to tell me what you hear him talking about while you're in his office. Phone calls, verbal interactions… notes stuck to his desk."

"Why?"

"Does it matter?"

The technician picked up his toolbag. "This will put my position at risk, and I ne-"

"No need to worry. You will be subtle, and in the unlikely event you're caught, I'll deal with it." He smiled. "And I'm sure we won't be needing to take up your workshop space any longer."

———

He went to Polly first. She typically came last. This didn't seem to occur to her.

"Your hair is different." Red polish was stroked delicately over her fingernails. It shone in the light.

The technician checked over the Dewbox, noting its operation. He'd fixed it only a week ago. "Not really, ma'am."

"It is. I notice these things."

Silence.

She looked him up and down. He didn't look back. "Is it broken?"

"No, ma'am."

"That's what I thought. I don't break things." She blew on her nails, then refitted the cap on the polish. "What was wrong with the Doctor's box?"

He paused to think. "Faulty wires. Like all the rest."

Her croaking sigh reminded the technician of cat woken from sleep. "Interesting."

He glanced up at her from over the top of his glasses. The toolbag sat beside the box on the floor. He hadn't even opened it. "That should be all."

She was flipping through red papers–white writing a blur. In the corner of every sheet, he saw the cardinal. "I'll have to test it out before I'm satisfied." One was removed from the stack, shoved into a folder, and swallowed by the Dewbox. It chirped its warning, then spit oil. "Fantastic. Like it wasn't even broken in the first place."

"It wasn't."

Her elbow knocked the polish bottle. It shattered and bled across the countertop. "Jesus. Clumsy me." She lifted the red papers before they could absorb, and set them on the higher counter. "Do you have a rag in that bloody bag?"

A zipper hummed. He reached in and rifled, finally finding a dirty cloth. It sucked up the red, leaving smears on the marble. "Should be fine. It might stain." He tried to fold it to find a clean spot, but it was all red now.

"That's what I get for not paying attention." She pulled

out a garbage can and snatched the rag. The glass shards tittered as they fell, covered in crimson. "The boss would have me whipped if I'd ruined those papers."

The technician glanced at the papers. He couldn't read the writing–too far away. "What's on them?"

She smirked. Her high cheekbones made it seem sardonic. "Never knew you to be curious."

"I'm not."

"Well it's important information you're too low on the food chain to understand." She paused. "As am I. I write them–or copy–and file them away. We are all instruments in the conductor's orchestra, Mister Becker."

"I'll be leaving now."

"So soon? And we hardly started talking."

A blank expression. "I thought I was simple, ma'am. How am I supposed to hold a conversation?"

She smiled. "How about that drink, Forrest?"

He picked up his toolbag. The soiled cloth was clutched in his fingers. "I imagine you have a job to do."

"Ha!" That was all she said.

—

"Sorry, Dewey. I think I busted it for real."

It looked ready to start smoking. The jaws hung

permanently open–rigor mortis. The technician peered inside. He ignored the sticker he himself had pasted on every box. *Do not look into the jaws. Detritus can be expelled at random.* "What did you do?"

"Nothing. Literally nothing. I was filing my papers, and it suddenly froze up."

"Did you file more than five at once?"

Silence.

There was another sticker, beside the first. *Do not file more than five folders at once. The jaws will seize.* A spurt of oil bubbled out the spillway; it was heated–frothing.

"Fuck." The technician peeled the tape off, fumbled for his screwdriver. "You have to read the instructions."

"Sorry, man."

"Yeah." He spit that into the cavity while he fumbled with the driver. The plate came off, and he saw the nest of tangled wiring. "This needs to be brought into my shop."

"I thought you didn't have one anymore."

Through gritted teeth as he felt about: "I got it back."

"That's great fucking news." He smacked the technician on the shoulder. "That's great, man. Really. Are you excited?"

"Sure am." He jammed the driver into the receptacle. The oil spurted messily, then stopped altogether. "I'll have this lifted down. I've gotta finish my circuit." Oil coated the driver tip. He pulled out the polish-covered cloth and wiped it clean.

"Sounds good, man. I don't need it today anyway. No filing."

"Fantastic." He dropped the tool in the bag. A pager on his belt received his request–sent it off.

Taylor watched with mild interest. "You can keep a secret, right?"

Silence.

"You're a good guy, Dewey. Don't tell anyone I said this, okay?" He unfolded his arms–folded them again. Nostrils flared. "I've been processing a lot of documents lately. I'm a curious guy, so I sometimes read a line or two… well… maybe the whole page. You wouldn't believe some of this shit."

"I don't wanna know." He zipped up his bag.

"No, really. There's faxes coming in from somewhere in Romania–"

"Taylor." He stopped. So did Taylor. "I'm just a technician. I don't care. It's none of my business."

The man blinked. "No one's listening, man. They're not gonna spike your coffee."

He fixed his glasses, picked up his toolbag. "I'll get your box back by tomorrow." As he was leaving: "Watch yourself, Taylor." His chest was drumming. It felt hot–he loosened his tie. The door clicked shut behind him.

He got a notice from his pager: *Box picked up. Should be down in thirty minutes.* The elevator rumbled. He imagined the cables holding his weight. One could snap and end him.

Ding! "Twelfth floor."

Metal rolling. The door opened slowly, revealing the red carpeted floors. On the wall, he saw the cardinal, perched inside the sun–a giant imposing grapefruit. He stepped out. At the end of the hall was the door. His footsteps were muffled.

Otis Lang, CEO.

He took a breath.

The glass clicked under his knuckles.

"Come!"

He turned the handle–it was made of gold.

"Ah. Come in." Lang sat at a black desk. Sunrise filtered through his blinds. "Morning, Dewey."

"Good morning, Mister Lang. How are you?"

"Just fine. The box is there." He pointed. Lamplight from his desk filled the lenses of his glasses. His slicked-back gold hair matched the trim of his blazer. "I move it around sometimes. Gets in the way."

"No problem, sir."

The box was fine, hardly used. The stained rayskin was marginally less stained than that of the others. Each warning sticker was unfaded–unpeeled.

"You still recognize your shop?"

The technician turned. "Sorry, sir?"

"Molina's a persuasive bastard."

Realization dawned. "Ah. Yes–everything's just as I remember. There's even some bits upgraded."

"That's my doing." He wrote something on a card. "New drill press… new circular saw–yours was busted–...new…lathe…" The pen in his hand clicked closed. "Consider it a gift… and an apology for stifling you. I won't make that mistake again. What would we ever do without our Dewboxes, eh?"

The technician forced a chuckle.

"You won't mind if I take a call?"

"No. Not at all." He set his toolbag down. There was no anxiety. He took another breath, and opened his ears–wide.

The phone rang a minute later. Lang picked up. "Good morning… Yes… No… Not a concern at all… I'd like the shipment at the end of this week at the latest… Can you-... Can you do that?... Good… It's on my desk here… yes…"

The technician glanced over his shoulder. Lang was fingering a sheet of red paper.

"Is that right?... Fuck... We have a plan for that... No... She's in stasis... Don't fucking pull her... Something's wrong, I think. Osian thinks so... Yeah... I will... Alright... Bye..." The phone clicked. He leaned back in his chair. "How's your home life, Dewey?"

"Pardon, sir?"

"No burgeoning romances, pipe bursts, kitchen fires?"

He rifled around for a wrench. "No, sir. Can't say so."

"Hm. My wife's going back to school. Economics. I think she should take business—help out around here." The glasses folded shut, clicked on the table.

"Yes, sir."

A pause. "You speak to me like I'm your superior officer."

"You're my boss, sir."

"You're a huffed-up contractor. I'm not your boss like I'm everyone else's." A cloud passed over the sun. The room darkened. "You saw Molina yesterday?"

"I did, sir."

"He's cold, that man. Don't let it bug you. Did he bug you?"

"No, sir."

"He's not too interested in you—or anyone else. His head's always down over a microscope. You'd think he looks at the real world the way we look at the little world through that microscope." The pen clicked. "We're two heads of the same coin. I tell myself that so I don't strangle him."

Silence.

"In fact, I have to run down to his office for a second. Just show yourself out when you're finished, Dewey."

"No worries, sir."

Lang got up and crossed the office. He fled out the door.

The technician turned to the desk, considering. He checked the room for cameras. Nothing—at least that he could see. He hadn't even pulled the tape off the Dewbox. It was fine—he could tell. He zipped up his bag, stood. It was only steps away. The paper was unguarded… But there was an easier way. A couple seconds pause—to make sure Lang was gone.

Then he left—quickly.

———

He'd screwed a bell into the doorframe—the kind found in convenience stores and little Chinese restaurants. It tittered as he entered. Light was misted through the foggy glass of the door. They'd written something on the outside.

Dewey Becker, Technician

He set his toolbag down by the door. They'd delivered

the malfunctioning box. It sat in the corner in the darkness–a skeleton. A computer hummed in the far corner. He looked at it, then at the box. He picked up the toolbag and got to work. An hour passed, and he didn't stop until the thing was fixed, then he tested it by shoving a file into its jaws.

"A Dewbox bleeds whe…"

It sat on a wheeled pallet. He heaved it towards the door, opened it, then slid the pallet and its weight out into the hall. His fingers nimbly typed a request into his pager. *Box fixed. Awaiting pickup.*

He locked the door.

The computer came to life and painted his face with color. It booted, then presented the desktop. *Cardinal Medicine.* He saw the cardinal in the sun–the desktop background. Everything was red. The cursor drifted over the redness, found an icon to click. *Dewbox Network.*

It opened up. *Admin Access to Dewbox Network.* He saw the files of every employee with a box. Any could be deleted, copied, or read. He scrolled through the names, sorted alphabetically.

Allan, Chris.

Brody, Taylor.

Harris, Polly.

Lang, Otis. He clicked.

It asked for his password, and he gave it. There were

hundreds of files. Every one of them of interest. He opened the first one.

BANG! The door came off its hinges. The technician turned around, saw a flash of red, then the room was filled with light. Guns. Pain in his torso. He fell out of his chair, but had blacked out before he hit the floor.

RED RUNNEL

He woke in a sweat. His arms were stuck–tied to a bed. Something tickled. He looked down, saw a needle stuck into his arm and a clear plastic tube snaking up to an intravenous bag.

"Morning."

His head could pivot, so it did. There was a dark shape sitting in a chair right next to the bed–ivory buttons on a waistcoat. He saw the glasses–the slicked blonde hair.

"Doctor Molina fixed you up. Those were low caliber bullets–didn't hit an organ."

"What?" His voice was faint.

"Rude, I know. But you wouldn't have agreed to this if I'd asked nicely."

"Agreed to what?"

"You know what. Don't play dumb, Dewey. Look around."

He obeyed. The room was sterile and white. Six gurneys

in neat order, all but two of them empty. His own, and one other–across the way, and too far to see clearly. "Don't do this to me. Please."

"If you start begging, I'll start to feel bad about it. Let me give you the run-down and we can get this done and over with." He pulled a cigarette from his pocket and flicked a lighter. The smoke danced across his face. His cheekbones were high–features rigid. Like a wild dog. "The Red Runnel. We sent two people in a year ago–a survey trip. One of them clearly enjoyed his stay, 'cause he didn't signal for extraction. The other must have gotten caught up with him. She didn't signal either. She's not dead–her vitals are functioning. When we tried to contact our first operator–Sonny Warren–our probe was… interrupted. A man was killed. We had to kill Sonny's body to try and pull him out by force. That didn't work. Now he's physically unchained. What he's done in there, we can't tell."

"I… what?"

A puff of smoke. "You're ex-military?"

"Yes, sir."

"Glad to confirm. You were sergeant major. I looked up your name. It's important we establish trust. You're good with guns? Technology? You don't shit your pants easy?"

"Unstrap me."

"No. You're going to save my ass. Why did you leave the

military?"

"Does it matter?"

"Depends."

A pause. "Because my wife was dead."

The cigarette smoldered. Lang looked hard at the technician. "You've got honor and courage, Dewey. That's a rare thing nowadays. If I thought you were at risk, I wouldn't be sending you in. Do this job for me—do it quick—and I'll help you out."

"I don't need your money, sir."

"I sign your paychecks." He smirked. "Would you like to know a secret, Dewey? I'll tell you, since we're building trust. I've sent forteen operators into the Runnel... Know how many came back?" He flicked ash over his shoulder.

"So I'm expendable."

"You're most qualified—and likely to finish this job." The smoke swirled in the lenses of his glasses. "There were commendations on your record-"

"-I forgot them-"

"-notes recording special weapons training. You're far more interesting than I thought, Dewey."

"I can't remember anything I learned, sir."

"I'm sure it's like riding a bike. Muscle memory." He dropped the cigarette and stamped it with his shoe. "You'll encounter things in the Runnel. Nothing immune to a bullet, but things that'll try and tear your eyeballs out through your asshole."

Silence.

"At least that's what we can surmise from the screams." Lang picked a syringe off a metal tray. It was filled with red liquid. "Incredible shit, this stuff. I'm sure we'll win a Nobel prize for it."

"Mister Lang-"

"I don't know if it hurts. Haven't gone in myself. Accessing a different part of your brain must feel like something. I've wondered if our ancestors had access to it–if they saw things that are hidden to us now. Maybe that's why we made such an effort to evolve–find a way to escape the horror of it. Isn't that a fascinating thought?"

The technician shifted. The straps were unyielding. "Why open that door?"

"Because someone always will, Dewey." He stood. "Find Sonny Warren and blow his brains out. Simple job. Don't be long." The needle pierced the intravenous, and a crimson cloud filled the clear liquid.

—

The technician woke. The room was the same. He still felt the tickle in his arm, and he reached down to gingerly slide the needle out of his flesh; it was followed by a well of blood. He slammed open a drawer and found bandages, wrapped them around his forearm. A dark stain tainted the white.

Lang was gone, but his chair was askew–still beside the bed. The technician reached down to grab the armrest and noticed something.

A pistol.

He dragged the chair across the room and replaced it under the table it came from. Then he turned around, saw the view outside the yawning window. The courtyard and fields were full of dark specks of life; they wandered upside-down like spiders on a ceiling. Gray skies were an ocean below, extending forever. He was dizzy. He fled through the door.

The cardinal in its sun was painted on the wall. Six doors–three to a side. He stood at the farthest, closest to the image. It was quiet, like a graveyard. *Click.* One of the opposing doors opened. Something began to emerge–a shape rendered gray, as if through the screen of a silent film. It was a man, with head hung low, and hair thin and dangling. He shuffled. There was no sign that he noticed the technician as he vanished through the main door.

The crimson carpet absorbed the technician's footsteps. He crossed the room, opened the main door. It was a hallway. Halfway down, the gray figure shuffled ignorant.

"Hey."

No answer.

"Can you hear me?" He followed, warily. Through another door. He recognized this room. The reception desk loomed in the far center. Now he left the gray wanderer and approached the desk. "Polly?"

She slumped in her chair. Her body was also gray, yet the corner of her mouth wept a thin line of crimson. It dripped from her chin into her lap.

"Polly?" He reached out to touch her shoulder.

Chunk... From behind came footsteps–redhoods. Their masks were smiling as they stuffed Polly into a black bag. The zipper whined, then the bag was hauled away. The technician tried to grab them. He wrenched the arm of the one closest. The bag fell from his grip.

"What the fuck are you doing? Are you drunk?"

"Lost grip on it."

The technician stood in front of them, waved a hand over a face. No reaction.

"Let's go, then. This isn't a sack of laundry."

He watched them go. He ground his teeth. He followed. But they were gone now, through one of many doors. There was one at the end of the hall, which he picked. It opened onto a concrete patio. Above him, people walked to and fro many feet away. Below him was the interminable void.

There was a pool.

And a figure reclined by the poolside. The water was like glass.

"Who are you?"

She wasn't gray like the others. Her bathing suit was blood-hue.

His soles clicked against the concrete.

Now she heard him approach, looked up. "You didn't take the gun."

"What?"

"You need it."

"No, ma'am. I… won't touch that thing."

There were sunglasses nestled in her auburn hair. She fidgeted with them. "Mister Lang left it for you. I think he's trying to keep you alive."

"He wants me to kill someone."

"That too."

The technician looked into the pool. He couldn't see the bottom. "Why… I…"

"I wouldn't think about anything too hard." A fly landed on her shoulder. She flicked it off with a red polished nail.

"Are you the… operator that got lost in here?"

"Nope." Silence.

"Then who are you? Why are you not… colorless like those others?"

"I'm your helpful little fairy, Dewey." She tapped her temple. "I'm up here."

He went quiet.

"This is the Red Runnel. Mister Lang pumped some R-Aspecticyn into your arm." She yawned.

"What's that?"

"It rejigs part of your brain."

"How do I get out?"

"Well, Mister Lang has to pull your intravenous. He'll probably do that once you've finished your job."

"But I already pulled it."

She pulled down the sunglasses. Her red irises could be seen through the half-tinted lenses. "So how about you go get that gun?"

"...No, ma'am."

"You've shot every type. Why so scared of a little peashooter?"

"You said you're… in my head. Why are you asking me questions you already know the answers to?"

She yawned again. "Have it your way." Her head fell back against the backrest and she shifted to get comfortable.

A pause. "Ma'am?"

"What?"

"What am I supposed to do now?"

"I already told you."

The technician rubbed his fingertips together. "I shouldn't be here."

She groaned.

"I need to get out."

Something splashed. He turned, saw the ripples. At the bottom of the pool, distorted by the water, something shiny spit sunrays.

"Go get it." She reached up to scratch her cheek. It was freckled.

"Why?"

No answer. The technician looked around. Concrete walls on two sides. Steel railings on the remaining—borders to infinitude. Chimneys huffed smoke over the walls. This was the top of the Cardinal Medicine building—except there was no balcony at the top of the Cardinal Medicine building. He said: "Goodbye, ma'am." Then he turned and walked back to the door he'd come through.

Ca-chunk... It was locked.

He went back. Her fingers were intertwined as she stretched, palms pushed outward. "You can't leave that way."

"Then how do I?"

"With that." She pointed.

Across the pool was a familiar object. The rayskin betrayed its wear under the scrutiny of the sun. An oil stain trailed down the side, connecting spout to receptacle. He stared with trepidation, like it was an altar to the devil.

"Feed it a file."

He rounded the pool. A file sat atop the Dewbox. The paper was crimson-hue. There was nothing written on it, but the cardinal was stamped in white.

"You're safe here, Dewey. With me. It's about the only place you will be." She blinked. The red of her eyes vanished for a millisecond—came back again. "If you want to talk again, feed one—any one." She lay back and shut her eyes.

The technician opened the jaws. They hungered for sustenance. He slid the file in, and they shut.

"A Dewbox bleeds when it receives a new file. Careful not to spill onto expensive equipment."

—

He looked up. He was in his workshop. It was dark everywhere, except the corner at the far back, where the glow of his computer shone red. His own box hummed quietly. Its warmth radiated. Oil spilled from its spout and traced the stain in the rayskin.

He wasn't alone.

Someone stood at his shop table, shifting lethargically

through the tools and junk. He was gray, like the others. The technician recognized the thinning hair, and the scent of cigar.

"Doctor?"

No answer.

He approached, peered over Molina's shoulder. There was a glaze over the doctor's eyes. It seemed his actions did not register in his mind as he performed them. The technician yanked a drawer handle, found a pack of cigarettes. His lighter hadn't left his pocket, so he flicked it and watched heat erupt from metal. The cigarette sparked and smoldered, and smoke flitted through the languid air.

Molina stopped. He turned–stared directly at the technician. His nostrils flared. He went back to searching.

"Doctor!" The technician bellowed as loud as he could until his throat was raw and angry.

No answer.

"Fuck… What the fuck is happening?" He sucked back smoke. It stung now.

A light passed by outside the door–red like blood. It was diffused through the glass–the backwards writing of his name in ink. The technician left the doctor and opened the door. Nothing. "Hey!" His call seemed to return to him like an echo.

Something sped around the bend in the hall. It was made

of fire and crimson rage, and every movement lagged and stuttered.

The technician slammed the door.

"What in the name of God?" It was the doctor. He looked up from the table, passed by the technician on his way to the door. Red light waited behind the glass. It could smell him. He turned the handle, and it slipped through. He grasped his chest and exhaled. The flesh of his face began to sag. "He…l…p…"

Thunk…

With a last effort, he pressed a button on his pager. Red glow.

The technician bent down. He could do nothing. "Doctor!"

No answer.

Redhoods flooded through the door. Molina was carried away. Dewey was left kneeling on his workshop floor.

—

The converted infirmary was on the main floor. He listened to the hum of the elevator—watched the glowing numbers.

4…3…2…1…M…

The doors groaned apart. Red carpet stretched off down the hall. Six doors. On the wall: the cardinal, overwatching.

He recalled which door he'd come from. It opened, and he saw the bed–the intravenous connected to nothing. He'd had company; across the room, in the sixth bed, a figure lay dormant. A woman. Her hair was as pale as her face–albino, yet somehow different. A file sat on the side table, half filled in with pen.

Roxanne Robbins. Thirty-six.

He couldn't tell whether the number was her age, or a designation. She wasn't gray. Her clothing was muted yellow–some kind of jumpsuit. The cardinal was embroidered on the breast–twice on the collar. An intravenous snaked up from her arm, its long tooth buried in her bleached flesh.

"Who are you?" The chair was still shoved under the table. He pulled it. The gun was cold. It was loaded–a nearly full clip, missing one bullet. A *Ballester-Molina*. "Jesus…" His hand shook slightly. He practiced aiming–peered down the sights. It came easier than he wanted. Once more, he looked at the woman in the bed, then he left the room. The pistol was heavy.

He'd kept the box of cigarettes. *Flick…* The air smelled of tobacco and gunpowder. It almost calmed his shaking hand. He didn't know where to go, so he went to the front door, past the secretary desk. Someone new sat in Polly's chair. It was a young woman–gray–writing sluggishly on red paper. "Can you see me?" He didn't think so. Something came back to him–a trick he'd tried to forget. He pulled the pistol out and aimed at the space between her eyes. Silence. He waited.

She looked up. A scowl. She looked back down.

The sixth sense of living things. The pistol returned to his pants. He went to the front door and opened it. It was all right-side-up now. The sky was up and the ground was down. Gray figures wandered to and fro across the front courtyard. Industry loomed beyond the property fences. In the far distance, skyscrapers rose like dark giant's candles.

He began to walk.

GOLGOTHA

All gray. Not one of them living–at least not to his definition. Some were police, carrying gray guns. Others were bums with gray beards. Callgirls with gray lipstick. The technician walked among them as a ghost. Occasionally he would touch one. They would react–brush their shoulders. That was all. Gray clouds drifted above through a gray sky. The world had lost its color. All colors but red.

He sat now, at a bus stop. Buses came and went, and the husks would lumber off and on. He never boarded. The *Ballester-Molina* imparted its coldness through his fingers. He pulled back the slide–peered into the chamber. *Click!* His thumb nudged the slide release. On and off snapped the safety. He stripped it–put it back together. He put it down beside him on the bench.

An engine rumbling. Another bus. It stopped, and the husks got off. The technician paid no mind.

"Blessed God."

He looked up.

It was a priest. His flesh was sallow, but colored. "You're here. Are you one from Cardinal Medicine? An operator?"

"I… Are you?"

"Am I? Am I what, child?" He smiled. The bus lumbered off behind him. "I asked you a question, son."

"I guess you could call me an operator. Yes, father."

"With protection."

The technician picked up the gun. He held it loosely. "I was told it's dangerous, father."

"From a wise man, then."

"A woman."

He laughed. It didn't sound real. "The fairer sex is often the smartest. Tell me, son, what you were sent here to do?"

"How did you get in, father?"

Another smile. The priest steepled his fingers at his waist. "There are other ways to enter, son. Natural ones. I am in touch with God, you see."

"Natural?"

"You understand where you are, of course."

No answer.

"Hm… Well, you haven't gone anywhere, son. You're still exactly where you were yesterday, and the day before that. It's all up here." He touched his temple. "Do you follow?"

"No, father, I don't."

"Will you walk with me, son?"

He stood–shoved the gun into his pants. "Depends where we're walking."

The Cardinal Medicine building was shrinking in the distance. Each step took him farther. He felt like a drifting ship.

As the priest spoke, his white collar bulged. "There are many of us here, son. The Red Runnel is not as much a secret as your patrons would have you believe. We are enlightened–those of us who have entered through nature."

"Do you mind if I smoke, father?"

"Disgusting habit… but if you must."

He flicked his lighter. The cigarette fizzled and spit.

"I am Father Ignatius." He wore round glasses around his neck, held by a string. "What is your name, son?"

"Dewey Becker."

"The operator?"

"Technician, father."

"A handyman. You hold yourself a certain way–a way which I have seen in my military friends. There is a certain gravitas afforded to those who have seen humanity's basest brutality."

"Yes, father."

"Will you tell me what you were sent to do, mister Becker? A military man, a technician–there are conclusions I might draw on my own." He fixed his combover.

"They're likely correct, father."

"You mean to kill?"

"I do."

"Is the man evil?"

"I was told so, father."

"But you have no further information?"

"If you can provide any, I'd welcome it, father."

"No, no…" He dodged a passing husk–a mother dragging a child. "I can tell you what I have learned since my enlightenment, none of which pertains to the judgment of good and evil in a place where such things are folly."

The technician frowned. "But there's danger here."

"Oh yes. Danger. Of a natural sort–not kindled by the heart of man."

"Do you know of Sonny Warren?"

"I can't say I do."

"Then I should leave you, father, respectfully."

Ignatius put a hand on the technician's shoulder. It was a locking grip. "No need. Stay and let me talk to a man who can hear me."

They came to a chapel. It was ringed by roads and warehouses. Smoke climbed into the clouds from out of brick and metal stacks. The distant mountains seemed more distant. This place was not natural. The technician was led up the small set of white painted steps. A painted Jesus looked down upon him; his eyes were gray. Rainwater stains made him weep.

"This is my chapel. Come inside, son."

The air was filled with dust.

"Who do you preach to?"

"Those who have been enlightened. They come from across the city."

The chapel was empty.

"Is there someone in your congregation who can help me, father?" He flicked the cigarette away before stepping inside. Christ was crucified above the altar. Many hundreds of wires held him airborne. "I wanna get back home as soon as possible."

"But you haven't left, son. This is your home." Ignatius stepped behind the lectern. His hands grasped the wood, and seemed to fidget for the bible placed there. "But perhaps there is one who might assist you."

Something sent a vibration through the floor.

"Is there someone here?" The technician looked around.

"Just the traffic, son. It shakes the place." He took off his glasses, wiped the lenses with the sleeve of his blazer. "Are you a faithful man, son? I'm curious."

The technician flared his nostrils. The dust was thick. "I can't say I am, father. I've seen no proof of God."

"God does not exist to give us proof of his presence. We must be faithful."

"I ripped bodies apart with machine guns. People are bags of meat, father. When you watch them die, you learn it."

Ignatius touched the bible. "You are a troubled soul. I think I see why your patrons chose you."

The pistol was cold. The technician kept his hand close. "Who can help me, father?"

"Pardon?"

Silence.

"Who? Who can help me?"

"What do you mean?"

"You told me there was someone who could help me." He felt a headache.

"Ah, yes. Forgive me, son. My mind is old."

Vibration. It shook the floor.

"Who is it?"

"Pardon?"

"The person, father."

"What person?"

There was a door in the far left corner of the chapel. The technician slipped through the pews.

"Where are you going, son?"

He grasped the handle and turned. It was locked.

"I wouldn't go that way." The wires that held the Lord groaned and swayed. The angle of his downturned, wooden head had him staring. Ignatius stared with him.

"Why?" The technician felt outnumbered.

"There is nothing down there, son."

Wind whistled through the chapel.

"Why did we come here, father?"

The front doors opened. Ignatius smiled. "So you might hear my sermon."

In came a swell of bodies. They weren't gray like the husks outside. These ones were colorless black, as if made of shadow. Widened, white eyes hung amidst dark faces—beneath the brims of hats or locks of hair. Their flesh seemed to crawl.

"Come, children. Sit." Ignatius motioned with his hands. "Find a seat."

Each would approach the lectern, and something from the priest would be sucked up into the formless dark. One after the other, each taking something—each finding a seat. Soon they finished, and the church was filled.

The technician waited in the concealment of the corner.

His breath was ragged.

"Now we're all settled, turn to *Romans 12:2*." A flipping of pages. "*Romans 12:2*. Yes, that's right. 'Do not conform to the pattern of this world, but be transformed by the renewing of your mind. Then you will be able to test and approve what God's will is—his good, pleasing and perfect will.' Yesterday I was riding the bus and as I sat amongst the unsaved grays, I began to think on this verse. We here are blessed, for we have been guaranteed a passage to heaven. Those unsaved are separate from us–and I'm sorry for them. But it is not our place to feel sorry, for it is in the hands of God to save whomsoever he desires."

A hammering in his temple–the technician blinked. The pain was growing.

"Now God works in ways beyond our understanding. He sends his red messiah to us here, and we commune with him, and through him, commune with God. There's not one among you fully transformed, and that is why you come to me. I am a son of the red messiah, and he promises to free all of you if you are loyal–if you are devout."

The wooden face of Christ seemed to darken.

"Now I ask all of you to welcome a special guest who's with us here today. He came here through means unholy, and I ask that you forgive him for it. He was sent by the devil to destroy our red messiah, and yet I sense in him a reluctance.

Perhaps our love and warmth will sway him." Ignatius turned slowly. A smile utterly inhuman split his sallow face in two. His teeth were wicked and dark. There were no eyes behind his lenses–only a blinding white glow. It illuminated wherever he looked. Holy light.

The technician pulled the pistol from his pants. His finger rested on the safety.

"Do not be afraid, son."

BANG! The side door rattled against the technician's heel. Another kick cracked the old latch. He slipped through, shut it behind him. It was dark. A stairwell. He descended– heard the click of the safety. His fingers worked unconsciously. He couldn't see. Out came his lighter, and a little flame formed against his thumb. It was enough to walk with, so he did.

"*Come back, son...*" It was distant, but close enough.

The basement was a maze of tall bookcases. Orange firelight cast strange shadows. Crosses were stacked against a wall. He ran to them and crouched down behind. There were footsteps on the stairs. Out went the firelight.

White glow–it bared the crooked smile, and the hooked nose. The darkness parted before it wherever the priest looked. He stalked amongst the shelves, throwing light at the turn of his head.

The technician's fingers were wet against the pistol grip.

"Do not be afraid, son." The polished dress shoes dragged through the dust. "I will save you."

His fingers gripped the slide. Slowly, they pulled. They met resistance.

Ignatius was somewhere out of sight.

Ca-chick...

The technician was blinded. He saw the smile through the light.

"M E E T G O D N O W."

CRACK! The smile was torn by the bullet. Teeth chittered against the floor. Ignatius fell against a bookcase and toppled it. A hoarse groan was leaking from his throat. He tried to rise again, and the pistol spit a second time. The glasses shattered. What light there was behind them fizzled and went dark.

Smoke whispered out the end of the barrel. The technician tried to steady his hand. The air reeked of gunpowder. He checked the clip. Two bullets gone. The safety clicked back into place. Fumbling fingers found the lighter again. He knelt and held it close to the priest's face. It wasn't human.

The lighter picked through the darkness. The stairs groaned under his steps. He looked out through the doorway. Empty pews. Wind gently pushed against the gaping front doors. Ignatius' lectern held a bible. The technician stepped onto the dais and lifted the cover. Pinched between the pages was a printed image. It depicted a crimson beast with skull exposed. Written in italics beneath was a caption: *The Rendering of Golgotha.* He shut the cover.

UNDERSTANDING

Bus tires rumbled against the road. He turned the pistol in his hands. Husks everywhere, in nearly every seat. None saw him. The hydraulics screamed. He turned to his left–felt the warmth radiating from the man's cheek. Hair hung over the gray face–wet and clumped, like it had rained. A cigarette fizzled. The technician sucked the smoke. He pinched it between two fingers–held it in front of the gray face, watching the smoke lick the achromic skin.

The husk sniffled. Looked around, then frowned.

"Have you ever shot someone?"

No answer.

"Didn't think so."

The husk shivered–rubbed its arm.

"People don't understand what it's like." He pushed his glasses up, scratched his stubbly beard. The magazine spit out. He checked the bullets. Five left.

The bus stopped. Someone got on–a transient man made

even more scraggly by his colorlessness. He reeked of crack and cigarettes. He stumbled across the bus in a daze–sat down across from the technician. As the bus woke from stillness, he slouched over and rocked with the movement of the tires against the road.

They got up all around him–tried to move to the front or back of the bus. The technician kept his seat and watched the derelict. Groaning. Not once did the slouching head lift.

"You must be lonely." He shoved the gun back under his belt. "I'm Dewey Becker."

Silence.

"I wonder what's going on in your head." The cigarette shed onto the bus floor. "Want a smoke?"

Silence.

"Hm. Guess not." He stamped the butt out under his shoe. "I don't know what's going on here, to be honest. Maybe I'll wake up… Maybe beside my wife. And every miserable year up until now will fade out of my head. But that's not how things work. I think she'd be pissed at me if she saw me moping around." When he looked up, his muscles tensed. The head had lifted. He peered into gray, bloodshot marbles. "Can you…"

Ca-chunk!

It was his stop. He stood. The eyes followed. The air was cold on his face as he stepped off. He watched the bus rattle away down the road, vomiting clouds of exhaust. Overhead, watching him, was the cardinal in its sun–wrought in metal. A front gate with gothic detail. The Cardinal Medicine building.

—

She was gone. The lounge chair was empty, and the gray sky reflected itself as a somber tapestry on the pool's surface.

"Hello?"

Ripples.

"Shit." He scratched his head, paced a circle.

She breached the glasslike surface. Her crimson eyes found him and stared. She had the slitted pupils of a cat. Slowly, she swam to the edge and lifted herself out. Now she sat on the tile, feet wading in the gray. "Back so soon?"

"Where the fuck am I?"

"He was a creation of Sonny Warren, that priest. Not human." She scratched her arm. "One of many." Water dribbled out of her hair as she wrung it.

"Alright… This is some kind of Hell, isn't it? I'm dead and facing my punishment."

"In a way, that might be right–abstractly."

"What does that mean?"

"You used to call me ma'am."

Silence.

She winked. "That little trinket I told you to get. It's still at the bottom of the pool–I checked."

He watched her sidelong. "I don't want it."

"You don't even know what it is."

There was no wind. The technician looked off over the railing into infinitude. "I've seen nothing so far to inspire trust in anything."

"But you trust me."

"And how do you figure that?"

"Because you trust yourself."

"I don-"

"-You trust a part of yourself–somewhere deep inside–to tell you right from wrong. Whether to turn left or right–chocolate or strawberry."

He sniffled.

"Your ego is still intact. Even after what it had to do."

"Is that right?"

Silence. Cat eyes blinked at him.

The gun clicked against the tile. He undid his tie and rolled it neatly–set it beside the weapon. His vest buttons slipped free, as did his shoes. He removed his glasses. "What is it?"

Her freckled shoulders shrugged.

"How don't you know?"

"You ask too many questions." Her lips parted in a yawn. There might have been fangs in her gums.

Hesitation. He jumped in. The water was tepid, and just as gray as it was on the surface. Something sparkled at the bottom. He swam towards it. It was cold in his fingers–metal, with a chain. Dogtags.

"Sergeant Major Dewey Becker... dishonorable discharge... murder..."

Water became a vacuum. It tried to crush him. Though he tried to ascend, his hands couldn't slice it. There was a low grumble, and the rattling of distant gunfire. A corpse–leaking blood. It hung suspended in the water. It was dressed in an American uniform. The technician tried to turn away. It spun around. He saw the face. It was screaming.

"Unfortunate." She was still sitting on the pool's edge.

He was fully dressed again–like he'd never disrobed. "Wha... Why did you show me that? What the fuck is wrong with you?"

"I didn't show you anything, mister Becker. Remember what I told you." She tapped her temple again and smiled.

"This is all in my head?"

"No. Not out there."

He ruffled his hair. The pistol came out of his belt. He saw her in the ironsight.

"That won't do anything."

He thought he saw her body tense.

"Shoot. It'll pass right through me." Her legs churned the water.

"I'm gonna ask you questions now." He flicked off the safety. "You're going to give me proper answers." She didn't respond, so he continued: "I found a picture in the church. A red skeleton, wi-"

"The Rendering of Golgotha."

"Yes. What is it? Why was it there?"

"You were drawn to it. It's the way out." Water dripped off her nose. "Or another one, at least."

"What does that mean?"

She sighed.

"Why do you appear to me as you do? Why a woman– why this pool?"

"Would you like me to appear as a frog? Maybe a horse."

"Answer me."

"Well it's obvious, isn't it?" She smiled. There were fangs, without a doubt. They curled over her lips. "You've lacked the companionship of a woman for nearly a decade. Since you killed your wif-"

BANG!

The tiles spit dust. She cringed away from the spark of the bullet.

"Don't."

"Four bullets left. What a waste."

"This is my mind, isn't it?"

Her fingers pried loose chunks of tile from the bullet hole. "Hm. At least you're starting to rub your brain cells together."

"I told you to answer my questions."

Cat eyes lifted slowly. There was a sudden weariness etched into her face. "You're letting it through, mister Becker."

"What?"

"The monster."

He felt sweat between his palms and the pistol grip. "I want to leave."

No answer.

The gun was heavy in his hands. He looked over at the railing–saw the infinite gray and the ground inverted above.

It felt like throwing a baseball, and tweaked the muscle in his arm the way a baseball always did. The gray sky swallowed it. Now his hands were empty. "Get me out of here. Please." He approached her and knelt. She smelled of chlorine.

"You're asking yourself for help."

"Please stop."

"Touch my cheek."

He grimaced.

"Touch it."

Her skin was cold. He felt the chill of it in his fingers, and the chill of fingers on his own face. It made him fall backward. "Did you… did you touch me?"

"No."

There was nothing he could do but gape.

"Finally, you understand." She slipped into the water, and didn't resurface.

The technician sat in silence. Across the pool was the Dewbox. Something had been placed atop it, though he'd seen no one else. It was the pistol.

A ROOM OF MIRRORS

Doctor Discovers Hidden Brain Nerve

January 1st, 1994

ROANOKE, VA – The scientific community is shaken this morning after the discovery of a previously unknown part of the human brain. It's being called the Aurora Nerve by the two men who saw it through their microscopes. Doctor Osian Molina, M.D., D.V.M., Psy.D., and his colleague Otis Lang, both founding partners of Cardinal Medicine, published a paper describing their discovery.

"It's a cranial nerve, we suspect," Molina explained. "One so small we'd never been able to detect it." When asked why it was so hidden, he had this to say: "Our best hypothesis as of now is that the nerve was affected by the same thing that took away all our tails thousands of years ago. Evolution made it smaller. Whatever it was responsible *for, our bodies decided it wasn't that important."*

Naturally, there are skeptics challenging Molina and Lang's claims. They await further evidence and opportunities to conduct their own studies to find this nerve themselves.

Molina went on to say: "Our own experiments indicate that the nerve can be stimulated. I won't tell what with—what's the fun in giving away all the secrets?" When asked what the nerve did when stimulated, the doctor said: "As of now, very little."

—

It was sitting face-up on a cluttered table. He saw the black-and-white printed image of Doctor Molina and Otis Lang closed in on all sides by text.

"A Dewbox bleeds when–"

Oil spit, ran down the rayskin. He hadn't used this box to get to the pool. This was a different room. An office– vacant, and stacked with boxes. He went to the door and opened it slowly…

… He caught something in the corner of his eye. It was hulking. The sound of squealing metal grew increasingly distant. Now it was silent. Concrete walls reflected dim lamplight; they were basement walls. Pipes snaked along the ceiling–one was labeled *SEWAGE* in flaking text. His footsteps were echoing. At the end of the hall was an elevator; its buttons were crimson lights. The top one was chipped and marked, smudged with dirt. He pressed it.

Somewhere far above, the building groaned and hummed. Machinery wept, and the technician waited. He pulled out his pack of cigarettes. His fingers crushed the flimsy cardboard–none left. It snapped hollowly against the floor. "Shit." Out came his lighter. Sparks caught into a licking flame; he felt the heat against his thumb. It puffed out. *Click.* It returned. *Click... click... click...*

B o o m...

He shut the lighter–turned around. The tail of the sound was still reverberating. It came from somewhere down the hall.

Boom...

It was metallic. Loud, but distant. He reached for his pistol.

BOOM...

Now he recognized it. Each sound was a door being slammed open–maybe broken off its hinges. The squealing he'd heard before entered his consciousness. It was coming.

Ding! The elevator doors rolled apart. He sped through and chose a floor–almost pounded the 'close door' button into the metal. But the doors wouldn't shut. His fist met the control panel, and a bright pattern of lit buttons mocked unhelpfully. He racked his pistol and aimed out the door… and waited.

Nothing.

The squealing had stopped. The technician listened to his breathing. He felt his nostrils drawing air. There was a different sound–human footsteps. Around the bend came a husk dressed in a lab coat. It lumbered towards the barrel of the gun, unaware. It entered the open elevator and made a face at the display of light on the panel, then it chose its floor. It sniffled.

He never lowered his gun. A dim lightbulb went fully out at the bend in the hall. Now he saw a shadow. It was there–unmoving, like a predator. Taller than a man, and distorted beyond a man's body. Just around the corner, it awaited a slip in judgment.

He'd never thought grinding metal could sound like music. It did when the doors sealed away the hall and the heavy cables lifted his metal box up out of the basement. The gun went back under his belt, then he glanced over his shoulder at the husk. It was occupied by notes on a clipboard. "It didn't attack you. You didn't even see it."

Silence.

The doors parted. He left the husk to its writing.

She was still there, just as he'd hoped.

Roxanne Robbins. Thirty-six.

He peeled through the notes clipped together on the bedside table. Most were scientific drivel. Others were not. *Lived with her parents–aristocrats in Romania.* It was scribbled in pen under a *Notes* heading. *Both deceased. No other family.*

Her face was placid–a mask of death.

"If I…" He touched the intravenous needle. Her heartbeat kissed his fingertips–it was tepid. A moment passed, then he pulled away. "Maybe you can hear me… you're not gray." Her lashes fluttered. "I don't think you're really here. You're somewhere else. If I pull this, you'll… maybe you'll go gray, or maybe you'll die. I need help."

Silence.

"I would've named my daughter Roxanne. Isn't that a hoot?"

Click…

The technician turned, saw the doors open. In came two Redhoods. A gun dangled from a strap around each neck–Steyr AUG's. Boots thrummed on vinyl flooring. They stopped at the foot of the bed–looked down at Roxanne through their masks. "What do I write?" One pulled out a clipboard and a pen.

"Her status. Is she breathing? Skin color, hair color, eye color… that kind of shit." The second one approached the bed. His gloves parted the woman's eyelid. The iris was blood-red. "No change. Still albino."

The pen scribbled. "Why are we doing this shit, anyway?"

"'Cause I volunteered us. Extra pay."

"Well, I don't have a science degree."

"You don't need a degree to write shit in a little box."

A click. The pen disappeared. "Isn't this important work? Where are the doctors?"

"This girl's been catatonic for months. We might as well be watering a plant. They've got other shit to do." Buckles twinkled as he stood up straight. "You done? Lang should be here in a second."

"Yeah."

They fled the room. He could smell the unburnt gunpowder lingering. Something caught his eye as he watched the door shut. There were papers by the bed he'd woken from. He crossed the room. His blood still stained the pale sheets, dribbled off the intravenous needle. *Dewey Becker. Seventy-eight.* Not an age, as he suspected before. Some kind of identification number. Paper fluttered. *Lives alone. Recently moved from Atlanta Georgia. Saw service in*

Vietnam as Sergeant Major. No attention if he goes missing. "Is that right?" It was whispered. He set the clipboard down. His own name smiled up at him.

Crack! The board splintered. He threw it across the room.

"Hard to face the truth, isn't it?"

He spun around. It was Lang, framed in the doorway. "What?"

No answer. Lang entered, bent down to pick up the split clipboard. He read the name. "This is Dewey, isn't it? That I'm speaking to? No need to answer. I can't hear you." He left the pieces of wood on a counter–walked into the center of the room. "I thought you would've left the building by now, Dewey."

"I did. What the Hell kind of pl-"

"But no matter. You're probably just figuring things out. It takes time." His panther eyes found Roxanne. "Ah. Maybe you're looking for directions."

The technician stood in front of the CEO. He looked into his eyes; they peered right through him. Shadows elongated every wrinkle in Lang's face.

"I see you haven't pulled her I.V.. Don't. It'll trap her in the Runnel and leave you helpless. It's four-dimensional, Dewey. I can turn around and see your body right in that bed." He pointed. The bed was empty. "But you can't, obviously. Our human brain is capable of accessing a fourth dimension of our world in which our physical bodies are… well, more or less separated from our… physical bodies. Hard to explain." He sniffled. "Think of it like standing in a room with mirrors on every wall. Each mirror reflects the other, and you, and every reflection of every mirror reflects the reflection of you. You're in one of those reflections now, and I'm standing in the room, except all my walls are covered by curtains."

"What?"

A pause. "Don't think about it too hard. Leave that to Molina and I." He smiled. "Speaking of… The old bastard had a stroke. Said he encountered you in your workshop–the way I'm encountering you now, of course. One of the Mites got him, I'd wager. Did you see a spawn of the devil that day?" He shivered–reached up to rub his shoulder. "Is that a yes?"

The technician took his hand away. He'd felt the fabric of Lang's suit jacket. Gray, cold fabric.

"Careful of those. Don't want a heart attack… or a popped blood vessel… or hemorrhoids. It varies every time." His fingers ran through his hair. "You'll find Roxanne somewhere else. If I knew where, she'd be out by now. I'd love to pull her I.V., but old Sonny's got some kind of hold on her. Pull the plug, her Aurora Nerve has a shitfit and grows like Popeye on spinach. That's not a good thing, if you're confused." He picked up her clipboard and scanned the papers. "Maybe your Dewbox is the ticket." After a moment, he set it down. "Just a theory, of course. I'm a scientist. Well… I did drop out. Maybe that makes me a naturopath."

The room reverberated the sound of a pager. Lang pressed a button and went quiet for a moment. He almost furrowed his brow. "Fuckers." A cough. "I've got something to do in this room, Dewey. I'll be staying for a minute or two. How about you check the room across the hall. We piled Sonny's shit in there. Maybe you'll find something useful–or meaningful. Directions." He waited, hands in his pockets. "Off you go."

He obeyed, reluctantly.

—

He crossed the hallway–opened the door there. It was some kind of morgue. Black bags sat atop gurneys. White tags hung from the zippers, each emblazoned with a cardinal.

Brody, Taylor… Harris, Polly…

"Jesus." The zipper whined. He saw her face and shattered glasses. They were still clipped to their gold chain. The aged skin of her face looked shrink-wrapped. It clung to her skull. She might have been a wax dummy. He'd seen it hundreds of times–the body without a soul. The zipper whined, sealing her away.

There was a jar. A skeletal, metal table was its bearer–empty of anything else. It was almost religious. He picked it up, felt the weight. Something was inscribed: *SW*. It clicked as he put it down.

CRACK! A hand erupted from out of the mouth, blowing off the lid. Cold fingers clutched the technician's wrist–*rigor mortis*. "Fuck!" He went for his pistol. Pottery crumbled against the butt of the handle. Out spilled a mound of ashes, and no hand. It was gone. "What the?" He felt his wrist–no damage. A cloud of human dust hung in the air. He thought he could see a face in it.

"What did you do?"

He turned. Saw nothing.

"What the fuck did you do? He was your friend! Your fucking brother! Are you insane?"

Humid wind licked his cheek. In the corners of his eyes, the ceiling was a canopy of leaves.

"Jesus! Becker's lost it! You're gonna get discharged, buddy! God willing, they'll give you the chair!"

"What happened, Sergeant?" It was a second voice.

"You know what happened!"

"Let him talk, God-damn-it!"

Silence.

"See! It was an accident!"

"Accident? Accident, my ass! He just blew Ricky's brains out! He's a fucking gook! Did they pay you? Threaten you?"

"H E B L E W R I C K Y 'S B R A I N S O U T." It was the voice of a devil. "H E B L E W R I C K Y 'S B R A I N S O U T. H E B L E W R I C K Y 'S B R A I N S O U T. H E B L E W R I C K Y 'S B R A I N S O U T."

The wind stopped. There was a Dewbox in the corner of the room. He tried to reach it. *Bang!* It sparked. Metal warped inward beneath rayskin. The teeth began to chatter, forming words. "A Dewbox bleeds when it flies through the windshield. Careful not to slip on my guts."

"Stop. Please." He turned the door handle. It melted through his fingers. "Stop!" The pistol was cold against his temple. His finger trembled against the trigger. He felt the heat–the bullet ripping his flesh, then the bone of his skull.

Silence.

The jar sat, unbroken, on the table. There was no Dewbox in the corner. The gun was still wedged under his belt. He took a breath. Under the table was a shelf–welded to the legs. He saw a milk crate. Its contents rattled when he pulled it out.

A wallet. A keychain.

He bent over the table, palms flat against the metal, head hanging. A ragged breath. He fixed his glasses–opened the wallet. Sonny Warren frowned in grayscale. *ROANOKE DRIVER'S LICENSE.* Behind it was a points card for *Rouge*. "Really?" There was an address. It wasn't far.

The wallet went into his pocket.

ROUGE

He opened the door to the converted infirmary. Lang was gone. Nothing seemed out of place. A glance at Roxanne–she still lay there, comatose. "What did he do to you?"

No answer.

He wasn't expecting one. The door groaned–latch clicked. Through the door at the end of the hall, he entered the lobby. *NO ENTRANCE EXCEPT BY PERMIT* was written on the back; time made the corners flake.

She was there, poking a keyboard. He approached the counter and watched her for a moment. "They'll kill you too if you don't do your job."

Her eyelids twitched as she strained in front of the glowing monitor.

"I shouldn't have pointed this at you." The gun metal nipped his fingers–cold. "I don't even know if I could shoot you. What would happen…"

A red paper pulled itself free from a printer's mouth. The

cardinal was inked in white at the top. She grabbed it and opened the jaws of her Dewbox. "A Dewbox bleeds when it…" Oil filtered down the side. Her chair squeaked under her weight. "Wish that technician was here…" It was mumbled.

"What's wrong with it?"

Silence.

He touched the rayskin. The tape had been removed from the side. Exposed wiring. Someone had tried to fix it– poorly. The solution was simple. He forced a misplaced wire. The box hummed, then sparked.

She leapt from her chair. s

"A Dewbox bleeds when it receives a new file. Careful not to spill onto expensive equipment." The jaws closed fully.

"Done." He prepared to leave.

Her fingers ran over the box. "What… How did…"

The front door opened and closed, letting in a draft.

—

Crimson glow painted his face. *ROUGE*. The bus huffed away. It was six in the morning. The doors were locked. He tried to peer through the glass; it was frosted–plastered with a large sticker. *No Minors*. A rock shred each letter–turned the glass to shards. His hand felt for the lock. Clear daggers awaited his arm. The door vibrated gently as he twisted the bolt. Humidity escaped into the morning air.

A neon rendition of a dancing woman was unlit on the wall. *GIRLS, GIRLS, GIRLS*. All was gray, like a memory. He entered the main den. Three poles on three catwalks. Empty chairs looked on in silence.

"Sonny Warren!"

Silence.

"Shit." He walked among the tables, checked the booths against the walls. Private rooms were all empty. The bar was untended. He found a glass and filled it with beer. It was warm.

Across the room stood a tall woman with angel wings. Fiberglass eyes were frozen in a sightless stare. She might have been painted gold; now she was gray.

He noticed a little box wrapped in cellophane. It was tucked behind the taps. Cigarettes. They shed their plastic skin. A lighter snapped and sparked. Tobacco smoldered, and smoke lifted over the bar. "Where… am I supposed to go?" He lifted the glass to his lips. Warm beer and tobacco. Like drinking from a urinal.

Movement.

Over the rim of the glass, he saw paleness. Wings. Maybe a bird. It fled into a back room. The glass clicked against the wooden bar–smoldered as the beer extinguished the cigarette. His footsteps were dull on the carpeted floors. There was a curtain. It screamed as he pulled it back. A wall. A poster. His wife reclined on a bed, her face rendered with printer ink. *I'll Please You. $400 Per Session.* The flesh of his cheeks went red. "You bastard." He tore the poster. There was a second behind it–a duplicate. His fingers rent the paper. Another. Another. "Stop!" He tore it again. This one was different. Her face was mutilated. *I'm Dying. I Kissed the Asphalt. $400 For My Coffin. $500 for the Service. $750 for the Grave.* He reached for it with a furious claw. Something grabbed his shoulder.

"Dewey Becker."

No one. The voice came from nowhere.

He left the private booth and scanned the main room. A woman stood on the middle catwalk, draped in white robes. Her eyes were wide–inhuman. They didn't blink.

"Who are you?" They drew him. He resisted.

"A messenger from God." Her human face peeled away, and six white wings emerged. The stems grew from a malformed visage made of fur and a hundred eyes.

The room was swallowed by the visage a thousand times, flowing like water through a hole. He tried to speak, but any sound was sucked out of his throat through his open mouth. His gun was unreachable. His arms wouldn't move.

"I am an angel. Be not afraid." Its voice was soothing. Like a singing mother. "Murder is a sin. Your heart is black with it." The wings spread wide. "In this den of infidelity, I shall cleanse the blackness. Your thoughts of murder will be wiped from your mind."

Behind the blur of color was a void of white. His hand crept toward the pistol. A headache. Every inch sent agony coursing through his skull. A finger touched the grip. He couldn't scream. Something tried to claw at his skull—from the inside. A connection was about to snap.

BANG!

He struck the carpet—groaned. The white void was gone.

"Hello, Mister Becker."

His bones ached. He pushed his glasses up. There was a man—standing where the angel had floated. The pistol lay on the carpet, barrel smoking—like his cigarette in the beer cup. He clawed at it, fingers stretching.

"No need for it. I'm not really here."

The technician sat up—audibly. He kept the gun in his hand.

"You bested an angel."

"I don't believe in God."

The man smiled. "I should alter my method, then."

"Who are you?"

Silence. He examined the technician with his albino red

eyes. "Sonny."

"Tell me what the Hell is going on." He got to his feet slowly. "Why does Lang want you dead?"

Sonny Warren strode to the bar. He sat down–glanced at the smoking glass. "Sit, Mister Becker."

He did–at a suitable distance.

"You're more level-headed than I expected. I have to apologize for trying to kill you so eagerly." His tone betrayed his education. His face couldn't be seen. A shroud of darkness followed him wherever he walked; his crimson eyes floated amid a hidden face–glowing. "This experience must be taxing on you."

A flick, and a spark. Another cigarette exhaled embers.

"But you handle it readily. A military man sees Hell before he dies, am I right?"

"Tell me what's going on." Smoke crawled out from between his lips.

"So much secrecy. It's an ineffective tactic from your superiors."

"Our superiors." He fixed his glasses.

"No. Not anymore." The eyes never blinked. "This is the real world, Mister Becker. What you do here affects reality just as it would out of the Runnel. But, as you must have guessed by now, others can't see you. It's quite a treat to toy with them, isn't it?"

Ash fell onto the bar.

"I've… severed myself from my physical body. My aurora nerve is now as big as any number of my other cranial nerves. I've returned to something closer to Adam. Made in the image of God, you might say–though I know you wouldn't. What I've done is break evolution. I've regrown a tail."

"They burned your body."

"Yes. They burned my husk."

Silence. Lights from passing cars reached through the windows–faded away.

"I'm not following."

"You're an inventor. You're a technician. I'm a biologist. I understand your flesh like you understand a motherboard. I'm as smart as Molina or Lang. That's why they sent me in here."

"You were expendable."

"Don't try to provoke me, Mister Becker. Nothing you can say would stir anger. I am beyond such triviality. I was expendable to them–that's not a lie. Look how it turned out." He leaned on the bar. Pale hands left their shadowy blanket. Albino pale. "Molina asked you to pry into Lang's business. You'll remember. Then the redhoods shot you. What do you think of Molina?"

"He had a stroke."

The laugh was short and cruel. "Molina's an old man. They kept him alive–saved his life. One of the mites got him–that's all. How do you think the redhoods knew when to enter your office and bust you?"

He frowned. Smoke. "I… They must have bugged my computer."

"Mister Becker." The crimson eyes were smiling. "Don't be so naive."

Silence.

"I'm such a threat to them. They don't understand me." A colorless face nearly crept into the light. "They would sacrifice anyone to eradicate something they don't understand. Something they can't control. That's what you are, Mister Becker. Expendable. Just like I was."

He pulled the smoking nub out of his mouth and stamped on it. "How do I get out of here?"

"The Rendering of Golgotha."

"What is that?"

"You have it still?"

His fingers felt for the paper. It was still in his jacket pocket. As he unfolded it, the crimson skull grinned up from the page. It drifted across the bar.

The pale fingers caught it. "A portrait. A dream portrait, painted by a dream."

"Hm?"

"You fled a monster in the basement of the Cardinal building. Did you see its face?"

"How did you know?"

"Look."

The paper returned to its owner. He took it up and stared into the face. It was a monster–an abomination of creation. He smelled the sweetness of decay–saw the mutilation of flesh against metal. It was a mask of death, a thing of violence… He saw… his own face–a mirror of ink. A gasp slipped free as he dropped the page. "What the hell?"

Sonny was staring. "That's your way out."

"Where… where's Roxanne?" He clutched his chest. It felt like his heart was clawing at his ribs.

"Roxanne. Sweet Roxanne. She reminds me of a song."

The barstool toppled. He struck the carpet.

"Mites are pesky bastards. Snuck up right behind you while we were talking. Hope you've got an aspirin." A snicker. The red eyes closed, and the shadow lifted. He was gone.

His leg struck the bar and the glass hit the ground. The cigarette fell, wrapped in warm beer, to the carpet. Every muscle flexed until he thought they'd snap; standing racked his torso. Frantic eyes searched the room for some solution– there was none. He stalked amongst the tables–a drunk, completely sober.

A light flicked on.

It shone onto the wall. Someone had drawn a chain in white chalk onto the doors of a cabinet. He grabbed the handle. Locked. "Fuck. How?" The hinges rattled. Another stab of pain. He doubled over.

The light flickered.

"It's fucking locked!" He rubbed at the chalk with his sleeve. Rage twisted his face. He kicked the door. It opened. The chalk was smudged–the chain was broken. Inside sat a small, white bottle. He took it and read the label. *Reteplase.* He felt it travel down his throat. Fatigue washed over, forcing him to the ground. He closed his eyes.

—

"Mister."

Cold fingers met his cheek.

"Hey. Are you dead?"

His eyes snapped open.

She was sitting on the carpet. Fishnet stockings. Her skin was ghostly. She was masked–heavy makeup. The whites of her eyes hung amid dark eyeshadow craters. "Hey… did you hide out here overnight?"

"What?"

"Did you get drunk and hide in a cupboard or

something?

He expected to see the bottle spilled beside him. It was gone. So was the cabinet with the chalk chain. The light still shone onto the wall. A half-nude woman basked in the fluorescence, her image laser-printed. "You can see me?"

"Yeah–of course I can." She frowned. "Jeez, buddy. You must be blasted."

She wasn't gray. He could see the hue of every patch ironed onto her jacket. He said: "No… No, I'm not." Wobbly legs carried him to his feet. He beelined for the window. The street was empty–early morning.

"Did you smash the window?"

"What?"

Silence.

He kept watching. Nothing.

"Hey."

"What dimension is this?" His eyes were wide.

She scoffed. A groan slipped out as she stood. She brushed dust off her legs. "I've gotta open in twenty minutes. You've gotta go." Her hair was a bob. She pulled bangs out of her eyes. "Unless you wanna pay for a drink."

"Are you the owner?"

"No. I'm a dancer."

"Dancer?" He checked his belt. His gun bulged through his jacket. "Shit."

"What? Do I scare you, or something?"

"No. No- Who's the owner?"

"His name's Richie."

"Is he coming in today? What time is it?" A finger pushed up his glasses. He turned back towards the window. Silent and dead.

"I don't know."

He went quiet.

"I don't wanna call the police, buddy."

"Why haven't you already?"

No answer.

The technician turned to her. His chest heaved deeply, then his breathing slowed. "What's your name, ma'am?"

"Audrey May."

"Mine's Dewey Becker. Now I need to ask you some questions, if you don't mind."

"Are you a cop?"

"No ma'am."

"Why do you have a gun?"

He pulled his jacket. It hid the weapon. "I was in the military." A second passed; she didn't rebut. "I work for Cardinal Medicine. They… they did some testing on me." A glance out the window. Nothing. "I don't know exactly what happened. No one could see me. I could walk around, but no one knew I was there. Everyone was gray. But you're not, so

I… I'm either out… or…"

"I'm gonna call the police."

"Yes! Call them! Please."

She didn't move.

"Why don't you?"

A blink.

Something outside made a noise. He turned and saw a man opening up his shop. The lights behind his glass sign buzzed and flared. A standing chalk billboard unfolded and was set firmly by the doorway. He looked across the street, then left, then right, then slipped back through his front door. His skin…

The technician looked back at Audrey. He pulled aside his jacket–found the gun. "Now you're gonna tell me the truth."

He clicked off the safety.

CENTIPEDE

Bang!

She stepped in the glass. Her boot heels crushed shards.

He chased. The front doors of the club swung back into place. Police sirens wailed in the distance. He'd tripped a silent alarm when he broke in. It didn't matter. Their cars pulled up–late. They strode up to the door, ignoring him. Red glow on their lifeless skin. *ROUGE*. It all vanished behind the street corner.

The dancer was quick. She weaved around the pedestrians–bumped one. He frowned at the empty air. Her perfume left a faint trail. It stood out amongst the moist gray melange. It always smelled like oncoming rain, even with no clouds.

"I'll shoot!"

"No!" Duck. Into an alleyway.

The technician stopped dead–turned left. She was hiding. He pulled the gun. "Please come out. I don't know what you are. Maybe you're dangerous."

Silence.

"I won't move from here." Wind tugged at his hair. "I'll wait for you to come out."

A car honked on a distant street.

"Ma'am. Please."

Two green eyes lifted over a dumpster. When they saw the gun, they fled.

"I saw you." He fixed his glasses. "I'll put the gun away."

She yelled: "Put it on the ground!"

"I'll put it in my belt."

"No. On the ground!"

He inhaled. Exhaled. He could smell her perfume–almost see it in the air. A red cloud. "I don't trust you. You don't trust me. Compromise a little. Please, ma'am." The pistol slid back under his belt. "It's away."

The eyes peered over. Then the lower half of her face. Her hair was mussed from the running. She slipped into view.

"Do you need a bandage, ma'am?"

She looked at her leg. The fishnet was ripped. Crimson–a rivulet down to her knee. "No. Well… No."

A junkie hobbled by her, then by the technician. He reeked of a hundred things.

"You're in the Red Runnel." He kept his eyes on her. "How? Are you an Operator?"

"I…" She went quiet.

He waited.

"I'm… Are *you* an operator?"

A pause. He sniffled. "I guess you could say that."

"You know my father, then?"

He blinked. "Who's your father?"

"Otis."

He blinked again. "Otis Lang?"

She looked at him quietly.

"Jesus… I didn't know he had a kid."

Her expression soured. "Neither did he."

A moment passed. "Why are you in here?"

"I've been here a long time." A smile, faintly. "Longer than anyone."

Another gust. It blew newspapers across the street. One sheet smacked the brick wall, then fell to the dirt. He never took his eyes off her. "What does that mean?"

"What do you think it means?"

He didn't answer.

"I'm not a stripper, by the way."

"I put that together." He wanted a smoke. "How did you find me? Can you sense me, or something?"

"No. I never wander far from the Cardinal building. I

was in the area and heard the racket you were making."

"Why don't you wander?"

"In case I run into one of you. So you can get me out."

A pause. "And how do I do that?"

Silence.

"Fuck." He pulled hair out of his eyes. "You know why I'm here?"

"My father sent you for something." She looked down at her leg again. Her eyes widened.

"To kill someone. He'll let me out if I do it."

"You know that? He told you?"

He looked down at the newspaper. "You know… I don't remember what he told me." He kneeled. The paper rustled in his grip. An adjustment of his glasses straightened out the printed text. *Cardinal Medicine facing injunction. Federal investigators suspect the pharmaceutical giant could be laundering hundreds of thousands of dollars to support research unapproved by the FDA. Dewey Becker is a wife-killing son-of-a-bitch who ne–*

"Then I'll go with you."

He folded the paper–tore it roughly along the seam. The wind caught it and took it away. "Alright. But if I sense–for even a second–that you're trying something, I'll put a bullet between your eyes."

She gawked. Nodded.

"You've been here longer than me." He pulled a cigarette. The lighter attacked the tobacco and paper. "Show me around."

—

Mid-afternoon came, and went. Commuting husks shuffled up and down the lonely roads. They hadn't left the skirt of Read Mountain. Virginia greenery flanked the highway–made gray. She led him down the sidewalk, hands in her pockets. He kept his hand near his gun.

Every movement she made was noted.

"Who are you supposed to kill?" She spoke loud over the passing engines.

He considered. "Sonny Warren. Do you know him?"

"No. Never heard of him."

"You've been in here longer than anyone… but you haven't heard of him?" He tapped ash off his cigarette into the grass. "Never seen anything strange?"

"Can't say so. Like I told you, I haven't left the area."

He heard a sniffle. "Where do you sleep? Eat?"

"I, uh… I sleep in vacant hotel rooms." She pulled her fishnets up. "I take food from wherever. That sounds wrong. Maybe it's wrong."

Silence.

"Is it wrong?"

"Huh?"

"To… to do that."

"To do what?"

Silence.

His fingers ran along the seam of his vest. A button was missing. There was blood on his tie–sprayed. Not his own. He searched the horizon for a smokestack. Nothing yet. "I think we should head to the industrial center."

"Uh… why?" She hadn't turned to look at him for a while.

He almost forgot the details of her face. "Because it's a landmark… because I don't know where else to look." Smoke from his lips.

"Shouldn't we look downtown?"

A pause. "I don't know. Fuck. I don't know–let's just go to the industrial center."

"Downtown has better odds."

"Fuck downtown."

Silence.

"I'm sorry."

He saw her head lower from the back. She kept her eyes on the sidewalk. The cigarette burned his fingertips. It flattened under his heel. "No. I'm frustrated. Don't pay attention to me."

She didn't.

———

Fluorescents shone through red-tinted glass. *SHEETZ*. It was hunkered there at the end of the road, backed by a steep grassy knoll. In the distance… the crown of a smokestack. It belched dark clouds into the gray sky.

"I'm hungry."

He furrowed his brow. "What? How old are you?"

Silence.

"I'm sorry."

"Nineteen."

"Oh." He padded his jacket. Nothing. "I don't… have anything. We'll stop in there."

A car pulled away as they crossed from grass onto the station's concrete bed. A bell jingled as the door opened; the clerk looked up, likely suspecting a poltergeist. He went back to his magazine. Printed on the cover, a nude woman covered her valuables with the body of a large snake. A sniffle. The page turned.

"Don't take too much."

She disappeared behind the shelves.

The technician looked around. There were bags of chips neatly stacked. Foil crinkled between his fingers. He checked the counter; the clerk was occupied. *Pop!* He couldn't see into the bag. It was filled with shadow. The sun from the window provided some light.

"He blew Ricky's brains out!"

Two hairy mandibles latched onto his hand. Twitching feelers lifted out of the dark, followed by a cluster of eyes.

"Fuck!" He dropped the bag, but ten legs had a hold on his flesh. The body was revealed as the bag fell away: a writhing length of scales. It tried to clamber up under his sleeve, but he grasped it hard. Pincers tore his skin as he pulled. It struck the linoleum, skittering for a foothold. His shoe came down on it, but he felt nothing as his heel touched down. He lifted his leg. It was gone. Potato chips lay strewn in the filth.

"God damn." A sigh. The clerk set the magazine down and went to find the broom.

The bag crinkled. He moved it around with his toe. Flattened it. There were no bite wounds in his hand, though he'd felt the pincers. Behind round lenses, his dark eyes traced the shelves–the stacks of chips. *Pop!* Nothing. No darkness–no insect. *Pop!* Nothing. *Pop!* Nothing.

"Good God."

He turned around–saw the clerk with his broom.

Bristles swept the debris. As the man got close to the shelf, he tugged on it–put some weight on the metal–

checked behind the bags. "What in the…" He shook his head, went back to the mess.

The technician watched him sweep. "Vietnamese centipede," he murmured. Audrey came up behind him, clutching a pack of cookies. "It came out of the bag. I crushed a hundred of 'em under my boot… back then."

"What?" She frowned.

A pause. "Don't worry about it."

They left to the sound of chimes. Some bills and coins now sat on the counter. Enough for the cookies—and all the popped bags.

SISTER

Night loomed heavily. Civilization had risen from the rural foliage. Husks swept the streets, walking home, or to some den of evening debauchery. Colorless glow from storefront signs caressed sullen, gray faces.

They walked amongst them. His cigarette breathed. She wedged a cookie into her mouth; it crumbled onto her shirt. "Frick…" A yawn.

"We'll rest somewhere."

"I can keep going."

"No." He stamped out his cigarette. "In here." A sharp pivot.

"An alley? Are we bums?" Her cookie packet was sealed with angst. "Is there a hotel?"

There was a manhole cover. He rounded it. "This is the hotel. I'm trying the back door."

"Why?"

"So I can find a key for a room. They don't keep them

out in the open." He tried the door. Locked.

"Can't we sneak through the front?"

He turned. His eyes flared behind his glasses. "Do you ever shut up?"

Silence.

"I'm sorry." Headlights grabbed at her from the street behind.

Someone started yelling, far away. The technician rubbed his fingers together, looked around. "Who was your mother?"

"What?"

He waited.

"She was… an office assistant–something like that." The night air tugged on her bangs.

"I just never heard anything about Lang having children. I've worked under him for five years." A zipper whined–his jacket fought back the chill.

"I'm nineteen."

"You said that."

"Maybe you didn't hear it."

He looked at her hard. "I guess I can't tell you to mind your attitude."

"No." She glared at him now.

He turned back to the door. It shook against his heel. He clawed hair out of his face. "We'll go through the fucking front, then."

She didn't wait for him. Her boots thrummed against the manhole cover… *Crack!*

"Hey!" He dropped to his knees–grasped the rim of the opening. The cover was gone–fallen in. A maw of darkness yawned in his face. "Can you hear me?"

Silence.

No ladder. He went in feet-first, hanging from the rim. There was air beneath him–warm and wet. His fingers ached. He couldn't detect a bottom.

He let go.

—

Board up your doors. Hide your women. Pray to God. He is coming for you.

It blared from the mouth of a thin, metal speaker. There was no sky. He woke on asphalt, cradling the back of his head. His glasses had fallen off; he looked around, saw them… beside a gray boot.

A husk–still as stone. It wore a hoodie and ripped jeans. There was a print: *Soundgarden.* Glassy eyes peered off into the interminable void. "Where…" A drawl–in slow motion. Nearly narcoleptic. "Am… I? Mom?... What… the… fuck… is… that?"

The technician got to his feet. He walked over–reached down to fetch his glasses. They cleared up the haze–let him see details. Its face was pallid and drenched. Sweat ran in rivulets down its cheeks, from its eyes–maybe they were tears. "You can't hear me… you-"

It turned. They locked eyes.

"Wha-"

Slowly: "Help… It's… coming…"

CRUNCH!

The technician gasped–stumbled backward. Its head lost its structure. Flesh and crumbled bone were held suspended in a sideways sweep. Blood took on a graceful shape mid-air. Time stood still.

Mozart… *Piano Concerto No.20*. It leaked softly through the thin metal speaker.

"I…" He fled to the left sidewalk. Storefronts and apartment steps ringed him in on every side. The road led nowhere. The sky was a ceiling, suspending heavy fluorescents. An instinct told him to hide; he ducked behind a set of stairs.

Then he heard the sound–the same he'd heard in the Cardinal basement. Wheels, creaking under a heavy weight. The beast appeared, as if God had placed it where it stood–out of nothingness. It didn't move–the sound continued. A stutter. Distance was gained. It froze again. It crept towards the husk. Pale flesh–like wet paper draped over a skeleton. Molding wood–the wheels were bolted to it: a rack, fettering the upper body. Motion came from the legs, which pulled the rack. A twisted cone was worn on the head. The neck was long, and crooked; it let the head droop forward. Stutter. It reached the husk. From the mouth grew a metal shaft, streaked with veins.

BANG!

The result had already been frozen in time–now the cause caught up. Fire escaped the barrel of the shaft. The blood lost its elegant pose, and seemed to recall itself; it painted the street and the storefront closest. Bone chittered against the asphalt. Flesh fell to earth. Then the body struck the road. Violins crescendoed from out of the speaker.

He watched with eyes wide. His chest thundered.

The beast retracted its weapon. Wheels creaked as malformed legs felt for purchase. In a moment, it was gone.

He wanted a cigarette. His hands trembled. He waited–maybe a whole half hour. Mozart finished his piece, then decided to play it again. The technician left his hiding place. Plastered gore. He looked around. There were no visible exits–only the doors to the storefronts. None drew him in particular, so he picked the closest.

It wasn't a store at all. The place was no bigger than a broom closet. Before him sat a metal desk cluttered with papers. Surgical tools waited neatly in bloody trays. He thought it was an animal–then he looked closer. A neck, split apart–then a parted jawbone. The nasal cavities were dried and shriveled in the mustiness. It was all cut and flared outward, like something had exploded in the brainstem. Metal pins held the flaps.

"Mother of God…" The brain was exposed–from the bottom. A web of nerves looked almost like computer wiring. He turned away, to a note on the table.

January 19th, 1989. I feel terrible, yet at the same time– invigorated. He donated his body to science… To me… I will love you forever, nephew. What a help you've been. I found it. In you… I'll win a Nobel.

There was no name.

The air reeked of formaldehyde. He turned, ready to leave. Something was scratched into the door. *This is who you work for.* The handle squeaked. He expected fresh air, but it was just as stale. His hand felt for a cigarette. One left. "Shit…" He left it–crossed the street to another door. White paint was slathered on the wood, forming letters.

Don't Knock.

Mozart stopped. He didn't play again. The handle jiggled, but didn't catch. "Hello?" No answer. A sound drew him–from back across the street. Quiet weeping. He crossed, climbed a set of steps. There was a window in this door–full length, with decorative facets. His breath fogged it.

It was one of the red apparitions–a mite. The room was expansive, but unlit, except by the peripheral glow from the overhead fluorescents leaking through the window. It was huddled against a wall, chin on its knees. It wept like a child.

"What the…" Something compressed his chest–a feeling that wouldn't dissipate. He turned away. His shoes clicked on the steps, then the asphalt.

Static vibrated thin metal. The metal spoke. "Mister Becker. Do you know where you are?"

He looked up. The speaker was bolted to a tall, withered pole. "Sonny. What are you doing to me?"

"Showing you something."

Silence. "That you made in your head–that you put into mine."

"Not my head. Not yours. We're guests, Mister Becker."

The corpse smelt like bloody beef. He glanced at it. "Whose head is this?"

"Use your critical thinking, Dewey. I want you to tell me."

"Where are you?"

Silence.

"Otis Lang's."

"I thought you were smarter."

"Audrey's."

"My God."

"Then who?" He could still hear the weeping.

"Perhaps you know, but you don't want to admit it to yourself. Is that right?" Static. A pop. "I think that's right. Don't answer me, then. I wouldn't think of troubling your delicate sensibility."

"Let me out."

"You can leave when you like." A pause. "Do you like Mozart? He certainly does. He listens to the same piece over and over in his head while he works." Sparks. The speaker went cold.

The technician stood silent for a time. "Sonny!"

A flickering overhead. Dust in the light, like snow.

He went to the door. *Don't Knock.* His knuckles struck the wood. Silence. It rattled under his heel, over and over again. He aimed for the spot beneath the handle—where he'd been taught to. There could have been cement holding it shut—no movement. Blood trickled down his fingers. He opened and closed a fist. "Shit…" He hadn't noticed it until now. Spots of crimson were left on the white painted letters. *Don't Knock.* "Fine. Have it your way."

A bird flapped its wings. A blur of red from one rooftop to the other.

There were other doors. He found one sealed by a combination lock. It was rusted, but the dial still turned.

"Alright." There was a dumpster in an alley across the street. He rummaged through it, trying not to stick himself with anything. A black plastic bag rattled the right tune. His fingers tore through its dusty flesh. Beer cans–hundreds. One would do. Back across the street, to the combination lock. He found the swiss army knife in his pocket, used his fingernails to pry out the knife. It bit the aluminum and sawed. He cut a tab, then cut the piece free. The mutilated can bounced away across the pavement. He wrapped the cutout around the lock's arch, slid the tab into the left hole. A twist. *Pop!* The lock hit the ground, shedding rust. He pulled the metal latch hinged to the doorframe and the door swung inward.

She lay there like a ragdoll–a woman he didn't know. Her clothing was torn and bloodied, and bruises tainted her cold face. Wide eyes stared at him, without seeing.

He entered, hand near his gun. Light from the doorway reflected in the pool of blood between her legs. A word was painted on every wall, over and over. *Sister... sister... sister... sister... sister...* There was a faint scratching. Eyes searched for the source behind dusty glasses. Nothing–just darkness. He glanced at the body, and froze. It was still staring at him... but he'd moved. He took a step. Scratching. It was hair grating on the wood–a lifeless head turning on a lifeless neck.

"Sonny…"

No answer.

"What are you doing?"

Outside, the speaker spit and fizzled. Mozart.

"Sonny! Answer me now!"

He crossed the room. Scratching. Her eyes almost rolled back into their sockets; her head craned to keep up. Now he was behind her. Blood trickled out of her mouth down her upper lip and into her eyes–up into her hair. Her head against the floor lifted her shoulders.

There was nothing else in the room–no reason to stay. He headed for the door.

Chick…. chick…

He fixed his glasses, looked over his shoulder.

Two large mandibles had grown from out of the bottom of her dress. They were still as death. When he moved, they dug into the wood floor and wrenched, dragging their attached body out from under the stained cloth. Spider. More legs, and tens of glossy eyes. There was no inflated abdomen–only a fleshy cord. It went taught as the thing came out fully.

The technician pulled his gun–chambered a round. Then he ran.

He could hear it skittering, and the sound of the load it towed. There was only one open door. He sprinted for it, slammed it open, then shut, and held it with his full weight. He listened through the thick wood. Skittering, coming closer. The door thumped violently. His knuckles were white.

It stopped.

Softer taps, traveling up the wall. A thud, near the bottom, then the sound of something heavy being dragged in pursuit of the tapping. He turned—saw the flayed head on the table. The notes beside it. *Nephew.* Everything went quiet. His hand never left the handle.

"*Raped mother.*"

He spun. Nothing. Nobody.

"*Raped mother. He did. He did. He did. He did. His own sister.*" The flayed head was gently convulsing—facial muscles forming words. "*I didn't come out right.*"

"What…"

Something stirred in the dark cavity where the brain stem was removed.

"Fuck… what the fuck…" Fingernails dug unconsciously into flesh. He loosened his grip on the brass handle.

Darkness took form. Eyes. Tens of eyes.

BANG! He twisted his wrist—threw the door open. It rattled against the frame when he shut it behind him. Wary eyes searched for danger—like they were trained to. The headless corpse still lay in the street. Lights flickered overhead. Mozart came to the end of his concerto.

And he saw the lifeless face above him, peering down over the edge of the overhead awning.

He aimed. Fire erupted from a metal nose. The pale face was pierced–bloodlessly. It slumped off the awning and hung suspended. Concrete met its paper flesh as its parasite left the perch. The arachnid clawed air to find footing. When it did, the technician had already started running. A great effort started its pursuit–the corpse was dead weight.

No other doors were open. He turned in place. Every hair stood on end. The fleshy cord was snapping like a whip–tensioned, then loosed. The corpse was filthy now, collecting dirt and dents. He aimed–the shot would be tricky. Iron sights chased the target; a finger waited on the trigger–squeezed until it locked… then further.

The fleshy cord snapped. Smoke leaked from the barrel. An alien screeching–the parasite flipped over and curled its legs. Black tar wept from the severed umbilical; smelling of rot.

Silence.

He took a breath.

The metal speaker fizzled. "I'm impressed, Mister Becker."

"What the fuck is that?" His gun was warm. It returned

to his belt.

"A regret—on the part of our host." Feedback vibrated the metal. "Or perhaps an accomplishment. I wonder which a man would most desire to lock away in his mental recesses."

He fixed his glasses. "I'm done here. Let me out, Sonny— or tell me how to leave." His hand was shaking. He wondered if Sonny could somehow see. "Don't give me a riddle or a test. Let me go."

"The key is right here, Mister Becker. At your feet." A pop. The voice went quiet.

Something told him it wouldn't speak again. He looked down—saw the corpse of the woman. Her eyes were closed now. Limbs were twisted and broken—bones shattered from being dragged so violently. There were no pockets in the torn clothes. He knelt. Careful fingers searched folds of cloth. Nothing. "Jesus…" One place remained. He gripped the umbilical. Flesh and tissue tore. Fluid filtered into the texture of the asphalt. It broke free with a start.

A key, stitched to the placenta.

Vomit tickled his throat. He looked away—tried not to breathe in. Out came his knife; it cut the stitches. The key was heavy—old fashioned. He took it and left the mess. The once clean street was now a massacre. He wondered whose mind this was.

Don't Knock.

The key fit. He pushed on the door, and it opened. He didn't look back as he slipped through.

RED WOMAN

A wall of odor–the stench of hundreds of thousands of people. It touched him physically, like he was passing through water. He turned–no door. It was a wall of glistening brick. Moonlight watched him through the manhole above. The ladder was rusted.

Cookie packet. Its crumbly guts were strewn.

"Audrey!" The sewer mimicked him a hundred times. He walked. There was a metal railing keeping him from falling into the mire. His legs fought him. Fingers grasped the rail, and he leaned his weight. Mozart's ghost plucked keys in his eardrums. Something whined–an echo. It sounded like a baby.

He expected to stare down into sewage. There wasn't any. It was a river with clear water. Chlorine and some flower's perfume smothered the stinking miasma.

She swam past–red bathing suit.

"Hey!" His heart was still thrumming. It started to hurt.

He walked along beside the railing, until she swam around a bend. Now he ran, took the corner… and stopped.

Her outfit was all red–head to foot. A peacoat, and pants. She studied him behind her sunglasses. "You saw the cruelty of humanity–but only in one sense. Now you've seen another. No guns. No war. Which is worse, do you think?"

"How are you here?"

"We haven't spoken in a while." She smiled. "You should come around sometimes."

Silence.

"Especially when you feel yourself… slipping."

He checked behind himself. Nothing. There were particles floating in the sunlight around the ladder. "What was that place? Whose mind was it? Not mine."

"No, not entirely. But your presence in it had an effect."

"What effect?"

A pause. "You can probably guess."

"Why don't you tell me? Save me the trouble"

"Now where's the fun in that?" She sniffled–brushed dust off her red coat. "How many bullets do you have left?"

He'd been counting in his head–pulling out the magazine to check it. Over and over again. "Two."

"Save one for Sonny Warren." She started walking. She knew he'd follow. "You have one left to use… and a long way to go."

Their shoes clicked on cement. "Where do I get more? I can't survive here with one."

"I'm sure there's a gun shop downtown."

"I'm not going downtown."

"Then I don't know."

Something was skittering. They turned a corner; she didn't stop walking. A bum sat against the curve of the sewer wall. Cans and boxes and wrappers and cigarette butts ringed him in, older and dirtier the farther away they got. Like tree rings–he'd been living there for a while. He didn't react to her footsteps, but his gray eyes tracked the technician.

"You wanna find Audrey." She buried her hand into her hair to scratch the back of her head.

"Yes, ma'am."

"You trust her?"

"No, ma'am."

"I'd have been disappointed if you did."

"Why?"

"Would you have been disappointed in yourself?" She paused. "If she weren't who she said she was? I seem to recall an event a long time ago… involving a shopkeeper and a little boy."

"Are you trying to upset me?"

"Just remember, Mister Becker…" She tapped her

temple.

They came to a dented metal door. Every conceivable thing had chewed away at the painted label. *MAINTENANCE.* The handle was gone. Light leaked through the hole where it should have been.

"After you."

He looked at her. Grunted. The door swung open at a nudge from his shoe.

A single bulb hung from a wire. Shelves held toolboxes and equipment. In the far corner… rayskin. Red stain. She sat on top of it, balanced her elbows on her knees–her chin on her hands. "It's not really here. In a physical sense." Her boot heel tapped the rayskin. "They'll appear when you need them. Helpful little things."

"I don't understand."

"You don't need to." She looked at him silently. Ten seconds. Twenty seconds. A snort–giggling. "You really are lost, Mister Becker. You should see your face."

Silence.

"I'm just here to check in on you. Make sure nothing gets triggered from that… encounter. How are you feeling?"

"What?"

Her eyebrows lifted.

"Fine. Why do you care?"

She smiled. "Fine? Good." The lightbulb was snuffed for

a moment, then flickered. The woman was gone. A humming from the Dewbox.

"A Dewbox bleeds when…"

The door slammed open at a push. He let it crash shut behind him. His shoes smacked the concrete. He stopped. The fetid air was drawn in through his nose–pushed out through his mouth. A whistle–long and labored, until his lungs were empty. Tension left his muscles. He walked on. There was hardly room to stand upright. Brick walls were lathered in grime; they were rounded. It was the gullet of the city. A few fluorescents lit the way for service workers. They began to close in as the technician walked. He felt the heat from them on his cheek. Offshoot tunnels carried waste water in. It trickled into the main runnel, every so often interrupted by some chunk or object. A needle. Used rubber.

He stopped.

A child. It was framed in a squat passageway, toplit by a lamp. It stared quietly. The face–Vietnamese. He recognized it.

"Shit." His hand reached for his gun.

Splashing. The child fled. The technician didn't follow. He kept walking.

It stared from around a corner, hands clutching the brick. *"Giúp tôi."* The lips didn't move.

"Cha tôi bị ốm." The head slipped behind the bend–

gone. Both phrases echoed down the tunnel.

He continued. The pistol was in his hand. "No. Fuck off! Fuck off, you little brat!"

Snickering. *"Cha tôi bị ốm."*

A storefront. It was built into the sewer wall. The doors swung open and he was dragged through by a little hand. A man lay on the floor between stacked shelves. He was coughing and moaning–exaggerated. *"Giúp tôi! Giúp tôi!"* The technician tried to crawl away, back towards the door. Some force yanked him by the jacket. His neck was wrenched–his eyes forced to look. The lying man was facing him now, a smile on his face. *"Người Mỹ ngốc nghếch."* He pulled a grenade pin–tried to shove it into one of the technician's pockets. Hands flailed, swatting the green egg. He got a hold of it–twisted his shoulder. It broke glass and sailed out into the sunlight. Out came a gun–not his *Ballester-Molina*. An *M1 Garand*. It shot a slug into the shopkeeper's skull. *Ping!* The clip leapt out onto the floor.

Screaming.

BANG! The child's brain fragments stuck to the doorframe. A man walked into view, dressed in forest green. "Good job, Becker." His *Garand* was smoking. "I hate bloody kids." He racked the slide and ejected his clip.

The technician gaped at him, tried to find a clip among his pockets–frantically.

"What's wrong, Becker?" He grinned. Empty eye sockets wept blood. The flesh was missing on the left side of his jaw, and the joint was snapped. It hung by a thread. "Don't wanna kill another brother, do you?" He laughed–gurgled blood. He spit a spray of crimson.

Silence.

An access room. A rusted ladder leading to a steel circle above. On the floor lay a dead raccoon–rotting. He couldn't distinguish between smells–it was all the same. The ladder… He could leave now. Sunlight was leaking through the holes in the steel cover; it was warm, somehow–even without touching him. "Audrey!" The sewer rang with his voice. "I'm here! Can you hear me?"

Silence.

He refrained from lighting a cigarette in the sewer. His throat was itching. "Why'd you show me that shit, Sonny?" A finger fixed his glasses. "Are you warning me? Or trying to screw my head?" No one answered. He looked up, down, up again. "Shit."

He left the ladder.

AROUND, UNDER, GONE

He was on fire. Running. His screams split the air. Around a bend. Gone.

"What the…" The technician waited. Kept walking. The smell of seared flesh and smoke was just detectable over the mire. Out came the pistol. A side tunnel, wafting black clouds. He forced his eyes around the corner–peered in. Water trickled down the middle–water and other things. The walls were soggy–almost reflective. There were no lights. He checked his rear; there was a large grate barring access to the opposite tunnel. No other option. He climbed in.

His shoes straddled the tunnel, shuffling awkwardly on the upturned floor. He tried not to touch the water. Another needle. A rusted nail. A clump of hair. The pistol skittered against the brick as he palmed the walls for balance. Flickering yellow light from the tunnel mouth was fading. There was darkness, and water. He felt with his hands–like a blind man. There might have been a curve. There was. Light.

It was another stretch of fluorescent–cloaked sewer. Water drained from it, down this tunnel.

A scream. From behind.

Footsteps–running. Running at him.

He clambered frantically forward. The gun fell from his hands. It splashed in the filth. He reached down, heart cracking against his ribs. It was slippery. His fingers struggled to clasp the metal.

He left it.

The footsteps drew nearer. His pursuer was right behind, breathing down his neck. He heard whispering–through manic breathing. He couldn't distinguish words. His feet slipped on the brick floor. A leg was submerged, but he yanked it out. Both shoes found footing, and he stood to face the tunnel's maw, which he'd just been spit from.

Nothing.

"Fuck." He blinked.

Iron bars. They were closed teeth. He grabbed them and wrenched. No give. "Shit… Shit! Shit! Shit!" He kicked. Threw his weight against the bars. He knew his shoulder would bruise. He slunk against the wall. The shit water was in his shoe, up his pants. What time it was outside was a mystery. It could have been midday, or midday of the day after. He closed his eyes–just to rest.

And fell asleep.

—

"I love her."

His eyelids split. No one. The voice was being played somewhere.

"As a sister. Any boy loves his sister."

There was grit on the floor. It stuck to his cheek. He brushed it with his fingers.

"Her flesh is like porcelain."

No speakers. No audio players. It was drifting over to him from the left. He stood like a doe–followed the sound.

"Her hair is a dark blanket–one I might clutch tight in sleep."

He felt naked. He'd been taught how to move through a space with no gun. His breath crept silent out of his nose. Around the bend was a steel door. He approached.

"Her warmth comforts me when I embrace her."

The handle turned. He entered. It was a cramped space, reeking of burnt flesh. Dead against the wall, a Redhood smoldered. The burning man. A table was butted up against the back wall. Printer paper was taped to an effigy made of sticks–humanoid. A doll, with the printed face of Doctor Osian Molina. Crammed into the chest was a small voice recorder.

"She won't tell mother. I told her I'd cut her tongue out. She won't tell anyone."

It was a young man's voice. Familiar.

"I know she loves me. I doubt I needed to threaten her. I'd never do it again if she told, of course. Why would she want that?"

There was something else on the ground, beside the Redhood. A gun. He reached down. It was strapped; it slung over his shoulder. The clip was empty. *Click!* The front grip unfolded. He checked the scope. A *Steyr AUG.*

"I see her stomach. It's inflating. I'll tell her what to say. She's overeating."

A note was rolled up in the corpse's pocket: *Your friend has bullets for you. All you have to do is find her. SW.*

The voice recording reached its end. *"I love her."* And turned off.

"What is this, Sonny?"

No answer.

He picked up the effigy. The doctor's eyes were dark. In this distance, a baby wept and screamed… or maybe it was a pipe creaking. It was made of plastic, the recorder. He slid it out from the doll. The sticks caved in—crumbled to pieces. There were buttons. He pressed one, then another.

"They don't know. They think she went out with some boy from school. This couldn't have gone better. Even after

father beats her, she won't tell. I think he suspects something, but he has no proof of it. This can b-"

He pressed a button.

"...vomiting blood..."

Another button.

"...not my fault. The baby died with her. It came out all bloody and disfigured. My mother blames the devil. I'm a man of science, but maybe it was the devil who had some part. I loved her."

There were no more recordings. He put it down on the table. The rifle swung around to his back; it was a hunk of useless plastic without bullets. It would weigh him down—he had no choice. He prepared to leave, saw a newspaper article thumbtacked to a corkboard on the wall. *A Blow to Modern Medicine.* Paragraphs beneath the photo of a man: *The revered Doctor Santiago Molina was found dead in his Roanoke Virginia home yesterday morning. An autopsy found large amounts of amphetamine in his system—the kind found in prescription medications like Adderall and Ritalin.* The rest was torn off.

"I get it, you son-of-a-bitch." The technician looked up at the ceiling. No cameras, no speakers. But he felt eyes on him, staring from some far off place. "But I don't know if it's real. Maybe you made this shit up." He glanced back at the article. The writing was different. *No, Mister Becker.*

He turned the handle and left the room.

—

A maintenance crew drifted ahead. Gray silhouettes moved against the backdrop of bricks. Some lugged tools–others clipboards. He followed them, a good distance away, so they wouldn't hear his footsteps. Not that it would matter.

Voices plinked against the walls, back and forth. Light. It caressed the wetness of the bricks. He turned a corner–saw a yawning maw, and daylight behind the metal teeth. A key. It turned, clicked, and opened the bars. There were no other tunnels–no other paths to follow. He sprinted, pushed past them. They grumbled in bafflement. Sunlight warmed his sopping skin. His clothes reeked–human waste. Two slopes of grass, left and right, walled him in. He climbed onto the highway.

Shoom! Cars. They rocketed past–blurs of color. A threat of tears pushed at his chest and throat. He didn't let them come. A finger pushed up his glasses. Out came the final cigarette. It caught flame, smoldered. Smoke filtered out his nostrils–blew out his mouth. The mountainous horizon offered him the smokestack–the industrial center. He could see the tendrils of smog now, waving.

"Made it out, I see." An oak tree's shade was his veil–

darker than it should have been.

The technician searched for facial features. There were only red eyes. "Where's Audrey?"

"Still on about the girl." A pause. "Don't you listen to yourself?"

"Tell me."

"In a second. I want to know where your head is. Figuratively, mind you." Red eyes smiled.

A puff of smoke. "Never been better."

"You understand what you saw?"

"Why not just explain it to me?"

Tires hit a puddle. They misted the roadside grass. Sonny said: "You think I made all that up? No, no, Mister Becker… I didn't make up a thing. Molina's got quite a mind."

"Is he hooked up? Like me?"

A pause. "No."

"Then how could I get into his head?"

Sonny never shifted an inch. "I can put you there."

"What?" More smoke.

"I can do things to the world, Mister Becker, and the minds of people. Stop death… erase a skyscraper… kill with a thought."

"Why don't you, then?"

Silence.

"Huh? Why not?"

"You're right. Why not?" He blinked, vanishing completely for a microsecond. "A man possessed of the will for world domination, or a perverted lust for human torture might enjoy swapping places with me."

The technician chuckled, huffing clouds. Orange embers fell to the asphalt. "I feel pretty tortured."

"Hardly. There weren't pills in that bordello. No cabinet with a chalk chain."

A frown. "I don't think I follow."

"Osian Molina is a monster. He and Otis Lang plan to sell gallons of R-Aspecticyn to the United States military. They're monstrous enough having discovered the thing in the first place and not kept silent. Do you follow now, Mister Becker?"

He adjusted the gun strap. "I think you're an animal in a corner, Sonny."

"Do you really? I have two options with you, Mister Becker. I've killed a dozen Operators sent in to eradicate me. They wouldn't listen. Fucking simple minds. Your mind is not simple. I ask that you listen to me. Roxanne will tell you the same."

"Roxanne? And where's Roxanne?"

"You have to agree to work with me."

Silence.

"Are you blind, Mister Becker? Do you think you dreamt

everything you just saw?"

"I hope I'm dreaming this whole thing. I hope those Redhoods killed me when they breached my office."

The tree shook, shedding leaves. "Wouldn't that be lucky? The easy road."

"You're god-damn right." He stamped out the cigarette. "I'll get out of here if I do my job. What'll I get for listening to you? My bet's jack-shit."

"Who told you your freedom was guaranteed? Otis Lang?"

A car horn blared.

"Don't be a grunt, Mister Becker. Use your head."

"I've always been a grunt. I'm good at it." He turned away—started walking down the highway.

"She's not that way."

He stopped.

"In there." A pointing finger. It was aimed at a gray hunk of a building. *VIRGINIA MEAT PACKING SOLUTIONS.* "Hurry up and find your bullets. They'll make this easier." Another blink. This time, they didn't reopen. Sonny was gone.

PIGS

It reeked of blood.

A dark hallway. The lights were turned off. Humming was deafening, coming from around the bend. Frames marched along on the walls, each trapping black and white images and paragraphs of text behind glass. *Virginia Meat Packing Solutions was built on a foundation of quality and family. Our product is the cleanest and highest-value in the country.* He crept one eye past the corner. White walls. Fluorescents. A vinyl floor with the hue of dried blood. Hulking doors hung on steel hinges, each with a singular glass eye. Windows, looking in.

His hair was disheveled. He pushed it back out of his face. A door opened.

A short woman, hispanic, with her hair in a net. She yanked hard on a rolling cart, drawing it out into the hall. The pig was bisected. Its ribs flayed. Flies circled; she swatted at them, then opened another door. She and the cart went through—so did the technician.

Husks stood at their assigned stations, pulling animals to pieces. Sterile white, splattered red. He broke away from the woman and walked in. Against the desaturation of the world, the liquid life of dead things stood out like lamplight. Red. Conveyor belts covered in it. Drains in the floor drank it greedily. Knives rose and fell mechanically. Heads and guts on one belt—edible meat on the other.

"Audrey!" He walked along the rows, peering down each. No answer. He could barely hear anything. The belts were screaming.

Another door. He gripped it, pulled. Stopped himself mid-step. On the other side was a shadowy drop—an elevator shaft, with no elevator. Cables dangled from the darkness above. He looked up, down... there were lights at the bottom; the walls down there were rusted and rotting. Dead end; he turned around.

A commotion, on the belts. The husks didn't seem to notice.

The meat was pulsating.

Grunting—from pigs. The corpses shifted, then rolled off onto the floor. Trotters clicked on the vinyl. They smelled him. Death-clouded eyes found the intruder. Snouts split in two, baring angry, red flesh. Human eyeballs rolled left and right within two slits in the redness. The closest pig dropped to its stomach. *Snap!* Fingers. A hand pulled itself out of the pink rip. Another. A pause, then bumps formed in the back. The tips of fifty-caliber bullets poked free–spines from neck to tail. The hands helped the animal feet–made the creature faster, but awkwardly.

The technician counted at least twenty. They were closing on him. He turned back around, looked up, looked down, then jumped into the elevator shaft.

A whisper of steel.

Grinding of an axle, pressed upon by an immense weight. It was walking towards him at the end of the hall, pale flesh gone red in the lights. The face was grotesque, yet human.

He lay on his back. Slow movements got him to his feet. No escape up the elevator shaft.

The maw opened, and the veiny barrel extracted itself–cracking and snapping. A pause. It stopped moving–became still.

Silence.

The technician took a step. Another. A third. Faster now. The barrel mouth was growing larger–closer. He knew it wouldn't shoot.

He reached the end of the hall. The beast was gone. He spun in place, hands clenched. "Come back you fucker! Come get me! I'll rip your fucking arms off!" His shoes dragged on the concrete, then vinyl. A door yielded to his push. The air smelled like rot. Saws spun hungrily on processing tables. They tore through flesh and bone–human.

The pigs were human.

They wore green. Uniforms. Conveyors carried their bodies through the machinery. He ignored it all. He ran through the room–he knew the path, every step. Something was in his hands now. A shotgun. The jangling of chains drew his eyes. Above. A man hung from a meathook; when he saw the technician, he smiled, and a laugh escaped him. Then buckshot tore flesh from bone.

Further. A gook dared aim a rifle at him from around one of the machines. The pellets macerated the man's face, spit from the shotgun. He kicked through another door.

"Mister Becker."

He pulled up the sights, aimed between the eyes.

"I wouldn't do that if I were you." It was a man clad in medals. He sat behind a desk in a dimly lit office. Sunlight trickled through a set of blinds. "Not after what you did."

"I don't care what I did."

"You should." A photo was lain on the desktop. Headshot–a soldier. "You tore his face up good, Sergeant. If it weren't for the people who watched you do it telling us the whole story, we'd have never known this bastard's name just off of sight. Would've had to check the records–maybe fingerprints." A pause. "You can go to prison for life, Becker."

"I should blow your fucking head off."

"Why did you do it?" No answer. "Bloodlust? Did killing all those gooks get to your head? Make you crazy? What was it, Becker?"

His hands held the shotgun like it grew from them–a bone, never shaking. "He was questioning me."

Silence.

"Said we should… take the mountain pass. That was stupid; we'd be sitting ducks. He wouldn't fucking listen to me. Said he wanted to see his kids again–that my plan would get their daddy killed."

Silence.

"And he was getting the others to believe him. Manipulating them. He was dangerous."

Silence.

"Will you fucking say something?"

"You shot him while he was pissing. In the back of the head. They all watched you." Dust floated through the sunlight. The man at the desk had a grizzled face–wrinkled from screaming. "They want you locked up."

"I won't go to prison."

"Why?"

"I'll fucking kill myself first."

"And your wife?"

Silence.

"She's very beautiful, Sergeant." A pause. "Maybe we can work out a deal here."

"Like what?"

"Bring her around sometime. Are you understanding me?"

"I'll kill you."

"But you didn't, Becker."

"I'll fucking kill you."

"You're a free man, and she's dead." There was no expression—no blinking. "What was her last thought of you, do you think? I can only imag-"

The buckshot cracked the man's head like a melon. His body fell behind the desk. The technician rounded it, checking that the job was done. But it wasn't a man's body that lay there. He put the shotgun to his own chin and pulled the trigger, then blacked out.

—

He woke.

The sunlight traced warm bars across his face. Black flies circled the desk, crawling on the blood-stained papers. He reached down, felt the shotgun… and stood. His head was pounding. There could have been buckshot in his brain– it felt like it. But there were no wounds on his chin. He grabbed the desk, propped himself up. Peered around at the body.

A man. Head flayed by lead.

He sighed, relieved. His finger touched something plastic. A pack of cigarettes. It slid quickly into his pocket– after he'd cracked it and pulled one free. His lighter snapped, spit fire, and the tobacco smoldered. The smell paired awfully with that of blood.

Something in the corner. Rayskin.

He looked at it for a while. Smoke wafted into the darkness of the ceiling. "Sonny." He waited for an answer, and got none. "You're scared of me. You don't wanna die." A puff. "But I've gotta get to gettin'. I'm sick of this place– sick to death." He couldn't hear anything beyond the confines of the office. It could have been floating in space. "You can't change my mind." He went to the door, tried the handle. Locked. His eyes found the Dewbox. There was no other way. There was a file on the desk–red paper, white typing; it was already slipped into a folder.

The metal jaws parted. The folder fell between.

"A Dewbox bleeds when it receives a new file. Careful not to spill onto expensive equipment."

Something had taken the water away. The pool was dry–a pit amidst the tiling. Flakes were piled at the base of the walls. Roots crept through punched-out holes, snaking over everything. Her chair was smashed to bits. She was nowhere to be found.

"Ma'am!"

An echo.

"What happened?" He walked forward. There was singing past the railing–somewhere in the void of sky. Or maybe it was moaning–tortured and disturbed. His shoes came to the edge of the pool. Plastic grates around the perimeter gurgled and vomited ivy. He looked down, into the gray pit, and saw something. Fleshy. Pulsating. Shoes clicked on the pool bed–the shallow end, then traveled down the slope to the deep. It was bloody and raw. It drew his hand–his fingers longed to touch it.

"You've slipped."

He spun. Aimed the shotgun.

"Don't you recognize my voice?" She wore all red–her pea coat, sunglasses. "He's broken you."

Silence.

"You should really be stronger than this."

"Don't fucking tell me what I should be." Hair hung over

his face. "I wanna leave. I will if I blow his brains out. I'm done."

She never moved. "You've been told that same thing before. How did that work out?"

"Not the same thing."

"It is." She sniffled. "And you should put the gun down."

He didn't.

"Shooting me won't help you."

"I won't know until I try."

Her body grew tense. "Sonny isn't lying to you."

"How do you know?"

"After all this time, Dewey, you haven't figured it out." She tapped the side of her head. "I don't know anything you don't know."

Silence.

"Are you gonna shoot me, then? Break down the final wall?"

"What?"

"You're letting the monster out. The one that killed Ricky."

"Start talking sense."

"I'm the final thread holding on."

"Did you fucking hear me?"

"Dewey."

BANG!

He opened his eyes. She was gone. The shell was still rolling on the pool bed.

Squeaking…

Behind him. He turned, saw the mass of flesh had gained a form. A slender, malformed man was strapped to a wooden rack. A cone grew from his head—a hat, or a bone, like a clown. The mouth hung open, and the veiny barrel extruded with a chorus of snaps. Its eyes were fixed, never blinking.

The technician brought up his shotgun—pulled the trigger. *Click.* "Shit." He spun and fled, just as the beast fired a poorly aimed shot. It struck the tiles and pulled them up in a dust shower. Now it pursued, with speed. The spindly legs pulled the wheeled entrapment with shocking efficiency. It scaled the slope of the pool and caught up to the technician as he was climbing the ladder. Both feet grappled for his legs, but he slipped free. Another shot from the mouth barrel. It sailed off into the void.

It couldn't leave the pool. The technician went prone to stay out of the firing line. There was a grunt, then a violent snap—a gunshot. Blood fountain. He crept up to see, and saw an exploded head. It had killed itself.

Slowly, he got to his feet. He noticed the box at the end of the pool. Rayskin. A folder sat on top.

Squeaking…

He turned. It was coming out of the wall, like the bricks

were the placid surface of a pool. Pain. It screamed, clawing itself free. The head snapped around–staring at the technician. The barrel extruded between rotted teeth. Out of its gullet came a laugh–a baby's laugh, played through a gramophone, or a busted radio.

He ran, there was a door. It rattled at him when he tried to pull the handle.

BANG!

He watched his own blood form a sprinkle pattern on the wall. There was a blowout wound in his shoulder. It wept. "Shit!"

The beast was closing distance.

He noticed it hadn't fired again. It needed to reload. Now he started a lap around the pool. He goaded it. He waited for the pain.

BANG!

Lead bored through his side, just missing the ribs. Now he took his opportunity. The iron jaws of the box opened; he slammed the folder through. Oil leaked out the side, ran down the rayskin.

"A Dewbox bleeds when it receives a new file. Careful not to spill onto expensive equipment."

ROXANNE

"Human beings must be treated as if every action they take is in pursuit of their own destruction. It is–really, when considered. Oppenheimer could have neglected his research into atomic weaponry, though some other would have inevitably taken his place–perhaps someone with greater malignant intent. The debate appears often regarding time travel–and how most would travel back to Hitler's youth to slaughter him in his crib. A common response for this is to say that someone would take his place as dictator of Germany–perhaps someone more evil. Or in any case, someone from any country–we don't have to limit ourselves to Germany–might become a more vile dictator.

I myself have been asked if my research into the Aurora can be likened to these similes–more so to that of the atomic bomb. Trust, however, that I have already mused over this question–as you can tell–and have a response.

No. No, I have seen every angle of morality regarding

this. As I stated, every man, woman, and child must be treated as if they are chimps with rifles. Wrap each one in Kevlar, glue the triggers, and weld shut the barrels. Each step of my process in unraveling this discovery is undertaken with the utmost care."

"What if one of the chimps finds a saw—cuts off the end of the barrel? Pushes hard enough to unstick the glue?"

"Well, that's always possible... Lucky then, that I'm the one to discover this—the one willing to wrap all the other chimps in Kevlar. Another man might have neglected such a foresight."

—

"Dewey?"

Her hands were cold. She wrapped bandages around his shoulder—his torso.

He looked down, saw his bare stomach. The flesh around the hole was bruised.

"Just lie down."

Sunlight. It felt nice on his skin. There was grass under him. She pulled the bandages—the hole was covered. The bandages turned red.

"Dewey?"

Strong fingers wrapped her throat. A faint croak from her

mouth. The technician sat up, fighting the pain. Crimson spread, sucked up by the pale cloth strips. "You're not real."

"I… am…"

"Bullshit."

"I… found…this…" Her hand came up. A cardboard box rattled. Bullets. *Freedom Fighter*. A bullseye and an eagle ink-printed.

He remembered Sonny's taunt. Squeezed harder. "He knew you'd have bullets. How?"

"I… don't… know… Please… Dewey…"

The fingers loosened. Audrey fell to the grass. Her skin was bruising–handprint, from ear to ear. She coughed, sucked in air.

He collected the box from the ground, extracted the magazine. Full metal jackets; they clicked in, one after the other. "Cheap shit." *Click!* He loaded the chamber, peered through the sight. The whole gun was hardly used. "I've been looking for you for… maybe days. Where the fuck did you go?"

"I… fell through the manhole-"

"I saw that part."

"Then I… I don't know. Something hit me on the head."

"How did you get here?"

"I woke up in that building… I found you in the basement. You were shot. I found bandages."

The *AUG* hung uncomfortably from his shoulder.

"I'm hungry."

His eyes widened. "Do you even understand the shit I went through to find you? God-damn! I almost died trying to find your sorry ass, and now you start whining like a stray bitch?"

"I'm sorry."

He tried to stand, but couldn't. A moment passed. Traffic buzzed along on the highway. "What do you know about Osian Molina? Doctor Molina?"

Her eyes were wet. "He would talk to me a lot."

"What did he say?"

"I think he wanted to… convince me to take the R-Aspecticyn."

"No, no. Not that shit. Did he ever tell you anything about his life? His background?"

She considered. "I asked him how he discovered the Aurora. He said he found it in his… I think it was his nephew. He died during childbirth… maybe… something like that."

"Did your father ever talk about him?"

"Why? What did yo-"

"Answer the fucking question."

"Yes. He told me not to talk too much with him."

The technician went silent.

"What did you see?"

No answer.

She plucked strands of grass–occasionally rubbed her throat. Clouds formed overhead and wept. It was light–barely a shower. They sat in it. The world was gray–all the more, it seemed.

He lit a cigarette. The smoke drifted up through the rain. "We're almost there. The industrial center. Are you coming with me?"

A pause. "I guess."

Round frames glared through nicotine smoke. "Then get to your feet."

She did.

It was a hulking concrete mass. The singular smokestack huffed toxin into the sky. Husk-driven trucks putted in and out of the parking lot. A sign was bolted to the side of the building–red lettering. *Virginia Industrial Center.* Two sets of feet crushed gravel. They crossed to the front door, dodging the trucks.

The door whined. Voices reverberated inside–along with the clanging of metal. Husks. They hauled ladders and boxes and tools.

"Follow closely." He entered. The barrel of his gun hunted like a snake eye. Unknowing bodies performed their manufacturing tasks. Machines punched sheets of metal into esoteric shapes. Tubes. Angles. Forks. They passed a husk whose arm had been shredded. He passed it under the hydraulics. *BANG!* Mangled flesh was further jellified.

Audrey shrieked.

"Shut up." His breath reeked of nicotine. The gun smelt of sulfur.

A poster on the wall. *Feel unsafe? Don't feel ashamed to speak to a supervisor. It could save a life*. The scream of a buzzer reverberated. Break time. The husks abandoned their machines and shuffled off through doors. Silence. Only the hum of idle metal.

"If you see a woman… with a yellow jumpsuit. You tell me."

She nodded.

"Or a man. Or anyone who isn't gray."

A pause. "Who's the woman?" It was a meek question.

It received silence.

She tried to wander off.

"Audrey." He stood there, brow furrowed. "I told you to follow me. Do what I fucking tell you, understand? Do you want something to blow your skull out of your head?"

Her eyes were wet.

"Come here, please."

She obeyed, slowly.

"Follow me." His hand was outstretched.

A gust of air. A blur of darkness. Something snapped her up, faster than anything natural.

He looked around. "Hey!" The gun searched. Nothing. A door slammed open. He let it shut behind him. Sunlight stung his eyes. The building was a sprawling thing, breathing smog from its smokestack. He was in an enclosed open space, walled in by the building. Rusted walls, barred windows, erupted concrete.

"Dewey!" She screamed.

It came from across the courtyard. He ran. There was graffiti sprayed onto the rust of a wall. *Christopher is looking for you. I'm waiting in the main room.* Yellow paint– a discarded can amongst the weeds. He reached down to pick it up.

The cardinal and its sun.

Metal snapped against the poured concrete floor. The can rolled away. He continued on.

There was a heavy metal door, pushed ajar. Vines grew from cracks in the cement, up onto the door, grasping like fingers. Rot invaded his nostrils. Tears were choked out. A line of paint wound away into the dark. The same yellow. He followed, gun half lifted. The smell was getting worse. He recognized it. He'd grown familiar with it. It was an old friend returning uninvited. Around a bend, the paint shot off straight down the center of a hall. Sunlight clawed at the boarded windows, seeping in. Black flies whirled back and forth.

Skittering. He turned, pulled the trigger once. A mouse was eviscerated by lead. A shot to the head, clean through the ear. His heart was hardly beating. His breath came at an even pace. Onward. Now he had to cover his nose with his shirt collar. It hardly helped. He turned–the paint stopped dead. Across a ways lay a body wrapped in a yellow jumpsuit–at least it had been yellow. The dye had almost all been putrefied–turned the hue of mustard, or vomit. A smashed-in head was strewn across the ground. Teeth, bone fragments, hair. The flies swarmed in a dark cloud–all around the room. The technician pulled his collar tighter over his nose. "Fuck."

More graffiti: *You didn't come. We're leaving.*

"Turn around."

He put his finger on the trigger.

"Sonny told me about you. Put the gun down. Turn around."

His hand tightened on the grip. "Don't threaten me."

"I'm not." It was a woman's voice. Young, and trying assertiveness. "I just don't wanna get shot."

"Roxanne?"

"Yeah."

"I've been looking for you for… I… maybe weeks?"

Silence.

"I won't shoot you." He turned around, let the gun fall to his side on its strap. A rare smile cracked his visage.

She wore a gas mask. It muffled her voice. White hair was matted by the straps. "Dewey Becker… Right?"

"Yes, ma'am."

There was a slight accent when she spoke. "I've been watching you."

He frowned. "You can put the pistol down."

She didn't.

"Roxanne."

It was a *Glock*. Standard issue for the operators. She knew where to aim it. "Sonny talks to me. He told me about you–your past. Everything he dug out of your brain. Quite a head you've got up there."

No answer.

"You're one in a long line of idiots. Lang and Molina have been trying this for a while. But Sonny hasn't killed you yet."

Another wave of stench. The body was staining the concrete. He tried to ignore it. "He thinks I'll free him. He told me."

"Yeah. He does."

"I won't."

"Why?"

"What has he done to convince me?"

She paused. "He's shown you the truth, hasn't he?"

"And I'm supposed to take him at his word, then." He suddenly remembered. "Where's the girl I was with? Huh? Something grabbed her."

Silence.

Then moaning. He turned around, saw the body twitching in its puddle of decay.

"Dewey." Her voice. She was there, where Roxanne had stood. "Why did you treat me so bad? All I wanted was to help you."

His rifle came up. The metal was cold against his cheek.

Her head snapped backward, then forward again. Now it was Roxanne. *Snap!* Now Audrey. "I never knew Otis Lang had a daughter." She spoke with his voice. *Snap... snap... snap... snap...*

The *AUG* began to spit fire. A whole clip was discharged. He didn't stop until the gun clicked empty.

Then a hand grabbed the barrel. White skin—no pigment.

"That's enough of that."

The gun snapped in two, and centipedes slithered out from the open barrel. They crawled up his arms, his sleeves, and down his pants. Pained wailing burst forth from his chest. The hand clamped down over his throat, and he was carried through the air and slammed against the wall.

"Why don't you behave, mister Becker?"

He was pulled away, thrown to the floor beside the corpse. He could see the spine and meaty cross-section where the neck was now a stump. It grew teeth and started chattering.

"I've tried to show you the truth humanely. But you're a wild dog."

The hand grabbed him again, dragged him across the floor until his hands and face were bloody. He was lifted, made to face his attacker. White face, eyes red like blood. Albino.

"Maybe coming face to face will inspire trust." He laughed, and his eyes flared.

The technician was pinned to the ceiling.

"How many lives have you ruined? Hundreds? Thousands? Maybe more. Killed a man for disobeying you. Whored your wife off to avoid a sentence. You must have really hated that bitch. I can see into your head–how she nagged you. Called you useless and degenerate. You wanted her dead in the end. You got your wish, didn't you?"

He tried to speak. No sound came out.

"No, no, mister Becker. Don't interrupt when someone

is speaking." Sonny rubbed his jaw. His features were lizard-like–cheekbones high, and nose pointed. Youthfully handsome. "Perhaps I've been heavy-handed. You never know, with every new fuckstick sent in here to kill me, I have to adapt my tactics. Maybe one day I'll come up lucky." He reached up, grasped the technician's throat, and carried him at arms length as if he were a doll. Out of the room they went, and down the hallway. "Roxanne's been beside you the whole time–I imagine you figured that out. A bit of a joke on my part."

Double doors slammed open. This room was vast, with a catwalk along the perimeter. In the center, machines hummed in stasis.

"You're not going to run from it this time, mister Becker. Kill it, and we can get on with the plot." He heaved the technician over the catwalk railing. "And no. I won't give you a gun."

I D

Squeaking… wheels.

The gun barrel extruded from between rotting teeth, cracking and snapping. Veins pumped liquid up and down the shaft–blood, or oil, or something else. It smelled like gunpowder–and dying things. *BANG!* The bullet pierced a metal tank. Gas shot out in a cloud, followed by a trickle of water.

The technician hid behind a machine. His heart was thumping. "Sonny! Sonny! Get me out!"

Metal clanking. The albino walked along the catwalk, observing. His only answer was a chuckle.

Squeaking. Faster. The beast was running–or hauling itself, rolling its wooden rack. It ran into the machine, swiped with its legs, twisting its body to get momentum. Another shot snapped in the chaotic air. Across the room, the brick wall shed dust and embraced the slug.

He sped away, as fast as his broken body would allow,

found another machine to hide behind.

"Fight it, mister Becker! Or you'll run out of breath!"

He looked around for something. There was a power box–switches inside. He couldn't read the writing above them. As the creaking drew nearer, he sprinted for it. Each switch was labeled, all of them red plastic. *MAIN POWER*. It clicked. The dead room started breathing. Conveyors hummed and lights flickered. He heard metal striking.

Some kind of power hammer. It pounded rotating metal sheets.

Lead took a bite from his hand. He yelped, looked down. His left hand pointer finger was gone. Redness welled from the raw flesh. "Fuck!" It left a trail as he fled along the wall.

"The first hit! Sorry about that, mister Becker. But our demons do eat us up eventually." Another chuckle. He leaned on the railing, chin in his hands.

The technician reached the hammer. It was punching shapes–he didn't know what for. He waited, cradling his hand. "Come here!"

It didn't.

"I'm here, you ugly shit!"

The mouth cannon fired again. It was easily dodged. Then the beast went still. It awaited him, as he awaited it. Neither yielded. Wheels scraped on the concrete. The thin legs hauled the hulking thing at speed; it vanished behind a machine.

Sonny gave it a minute, then said: "Can't have this now, can we?"

The walls closed in at lightning speed, then the room was gone. Now he was in a hallway, dimly lit from the ceiling. Squeaking came from one end, then the beast. It was running.

"Run, run, mister Becker. Like you always do."

Shoes clicked on concrete. The technician bolted. Lights whizzed past in the reflection of his glasses.

"Ah, one of my favorite songs."

An electric guitar called from some distant place. *Roxanne*. The vocal plinked off the hallway walls. Sonny sang with them. There was another sound. Flipping pages.

BANG! The shot ricocheted off the concrete. A light sparked and spit glass shards. He passed through the cloud of darkness, still running. His lungs were burning. Every cough tasted like nicotine smoke. Behind loomed the beast. Its warmth radiated; he could feel it on the back of his neck. It smelled like a rotting summertime corpse. "SONNY!"

Gravity forgot itself. The hallway flipped lengthwise. He slid down the floor towards a set of crimson doors. They gave under his heels and he struck the concrete of the machine room—the one he'd just been yanked from.

Sonny sat on the catwalk, a book in his hand. The song

hummed through the ceiling speakers. "Up, mister Becker."

A heavy foot compressed the technician's ribcage. He spat blood. It lifted, came down again–and again. The life was being stomped from his body. The beast smiled widely from beneath its sunken brow and cone hat. Out came the gun barrel. It shed flakes as it snapped and crackled. Darkness was a metal-framed eye, ready to weep lead.

He grappled. Fingers wrapped the barrel, pushing it away. His arm fell, too weak. "Sonny!" He pushed again, just in time. Fire erupted from the mouth. The bullet hit the ground. He heard ringing in his ears, then nothing at all. Another attempt to grab. It was hot metal. It burned his fingers. He let go. The beast looked at him with wide, white eyes. Its jaw was overextended to accommodate the barrel. Saliva leaked from the cracks between lips and metal.

More grabbing. It was cool enough now. He pulled, let go. Grabbed again, and pulled.

The beast screeched like a wild cat. Blood spilled from its mouth where the barrel had been torn free. It snapped its human teeth–the tens of them, all rotting.

He threw the barrel away. The veins, trailing and cut, were leaking now. Both feet came off his chest, and he rolled aside, sucking in fetid air. Gradually, he found footing, and stumbled to the power hammer. It supported him–let him lean over in pain.

Another page flip. Sonny's eyes moved from the book to the scene below.

"Come here, you fuck." The technician waited while the beast writhed. It seemed to kneel over the amputated barrel and weep. Sadness turned to rage, and it charged, feet dragging the wooden rack faster than they seemed able. It tried to wrap them around his neck. He grappled the thin flesh, tore it and wrenched. His fingers clamped down on the head, and he used the rack's wheels to rotate the attached body. It fit just right beneath the power hammer–the wretched head. And it fractured under the impact. The body slumped, dead.

—

He woke in a chair.

It was a comfortable chair. His searching fingers found something–glass. Wine in a glass. A fireplace crackled to his right. Rain tapped against a darkened window. Everywhere was varnished wood.

"I congratulate you, mister Becker." He sat across in a second chair. The firelight cast strange shadows across his face. "Not everything you witnessed, and continue to witness, was a result of my tampering with the Runnel. Some things are made by those who are dim enough to enter.

Any demon which lives in a human mind can manifest itself, appropriately, as just that. A demon. As long as you're in here." He smiled. "Excuse my pontificating."

He turned, saw another body in a third chair. Her hair was pale white.

"Hi."

A frown. He checked his hand. Bandaged–one finger still missing.

"A souvenir. So you never forget yourself again." Sonny sipped his wine. "You killed your ego. That'll take some time to regenerate. But she'll return. Just visit one of your boxes."

"What's happening?" He searched for a cigarette. The pack was gone.

"You have one final test." There was a gun on the table beside him. *Ballester-molina.* "It's only one question. I don't think I even need to ask it–you already know."

"Is that my gun?"

"Maybe."

Silence. He sat back in his chair. Relaxed.

"What's your answer?"

He looked at Roxanne. She blinked. Red eyes. The two of them were aliens–he felt abducted. The fire crackled in the stillness. "What do you want me to do, then?" He shifted. "We'll start there."

"Molina and Lang want to sell R-Aspecticyn to wealthy buyers. I told you this–you know. Governments, cartels–others. Humanity should have never pried into the Runnel. We need to destroy the drug–all the research, and the evidence that it ever existed." He paused. "That's all I want."

He fixed his glasses. They were cracked. "Is that right?"

"It is." Sonny set his wine down. "Roxanne can be let out. You need to unplug her."

"Lang said that would kill her."

"Yes, of course he did."

Silence. "I can't unplug myself?"

"No. That would kill you. To come out, it needs to be a system shock–the brain can't know the precise moment it will happen. A conscious thought to expect the severing connection, while it's severing, will be like placing your brain between a brick wall and a semi truck."

"How will I get out?" He gripped the chair.

"Roxanne will unplug you from the outside."

"And what about you?"

"I think I'll be here forever, mister Becker."

The technician sniffed. "That's honorable."

"It's necessary. To prevent what will happen. I knew it the moment I cut myself from my body."

"And how did you do that?"

A pause. "Does it matter?"

"Yes."

Two sets of red eyes met, then parted. Sonny said: "I killed my body. In the Cardinal building. Shot it in the heart." He picked up the wine, took another drink. "I didn't know if it would work. It did. I watched them burn my body. Funny, I think, that their efforts only made it more impossible to accomplish what they wanted. They guaranteed my fate–beyond a guarantee."

The technician's eyes glimmered behind reflected firelight.

"But enough of that. I'm a dead man walking, you might say. I need to know, mister Becker. What's your answer?"

He sat in quiet. Then he said: "What will Roxanne do outside?"

She spoke. Her voice had a hint of something Slavic. The technician remembered her bedside file. Romanian. "I'll destroy everything. I know where all of it is. Then I'll burn the drug caches. Then, mister Becker, I'll unplug you."

"Maybe you're both lying."

Sonny smirked. "Maybe. But I'm not the one asking you to kill for me."

Spectacled eyes drifted over to the pistol. "Can I have that back?"

———

The bus was late.

He sat on the bench, field stripping the gun, putting it back together. Wind beat at his left side. Behind him, the industrial center was a dark monolith. Out of it came a yellow-clad figure.

"Mister Becker." She came up to the bench, hands in her jumpsuit pockets. "I'm sorry I dropped that packet of cookies you bought. Waste of money."

The gun clicked and snapped. "Tell me, ma'am–truly now. Is he lying to me?"

Her eyes narrowed. "No, mister Becker. He's not. He can only make this place as evil as the operators think. Do you understand me? Everything you saw–and I have no idea–came from your own head."

"I saw Molina's sister. I heard a piece of Mozart I've never heard all the way through. That didn't come from me."

She sniffled in the cold. "You'll have to ask him about that, then."

"I'll never see him again."

"Then best forget it." Her boots crunched gravel. "Do you trust me?"

He paused. "I told you–your… body… that if I'd ever had a daughter, her name would've been Roxanne. Take that as you want."

"Flattering. You're not just a grumpy old fuck after all."

The corner of his mouth let a smile slip.

"See you soon, then, Dewey." She turned and walked back into the looming building.

He picked up the gun again, stripped it, put it back together. There was still a pain in his torso–in his hand. His body was letting him down. The slide pulled back, snapped forward. He put it down beside him on the bench.

Footsteps.

A woman approached–gray. He took the gun away just as she sat down beside him. She pulled out a book and opened it. Her eyes were empty.

"You look like Lizzie." He looked at her face. Her hair fell over her eyes. She couldn't hear.

The woman sniffled in the cold. She reached up to brush the hair away.

"Are you real?"

Silence. She flipped a page. Her eyes hardly moved–if they moved at all.

The technician touched her shoulder. She turned and looked at him. They locked eyes without knowing. She continued to read. He said: "You wouldn't believe what happened to me."

Silence.

"Worse than anything in Vietnam. But… Vietnam was real."

A page flip.

"I think about you every day." A pause. "I hate myself. I… would trade my life for yours."

Silence.

"I, uh… I never got rid of any of your stuff. All your… dumb little flowers. I water them every two days. They're still alive. Well… I don't know how long I've been in here. Maybe they're starting to wilt."

Silence.

"Remember when we would walk in the city. You'd always look at Rouge–that strip club–make that face. I went in there. I had to, I promise. It was just as much of a shit-hole as you thought it would be."

A page flip. She pulled hair out of her eyes.

"Lizzie."

Silence.

"I'm sorry," he said. "For asking you to love me."

An engine. A bus rounded the bend. It stopped, and she rose from the bench, shutting her book. She boarded, and the doors shut.

"Goodbye."

A cloud of exhaust. The bus was gone.

WAKE UP

She sucked in air through her open mouth, sat up in the bed. Blood and R-Aspecticyn were flowing down her arm onto the white bedsheets. Her brain was thrumming against her skull. The room spun. She collapsed onto the floor. A cough. More of the drug misted, spilled from her nose–was cried from her tear ducts. She heard a sound from outside. Some kind of racket. She lay there, leaking, for what felt like hours.

Then her strength started to return. Enough, at least, to stand up. Yellow combat boots–the same hue as her jumpsuit–found unsteady footing. She examined the room. Same as she remembered–with little changes. Dewey's body lay in a bed at the far end. "Damn…" More coughing. It felt like her throat was tightening. The wet flesh swelled, making it hard to breathe. "*Haahh…. Fahh..*" Back to the ground. She rolled to her side, rubbing her throat, pulling her hair, writhing. Tears ran down her colorless cheeks. They were red–mixed with the drug. She sobbed, and came to rest on her back, legs unconsciously occupied in a slow kicking–like she was treading water. Vomit came next; it *slomped* from out of her lips, onto the tiles. Red. Blood, and medicine. Her chest contracted, and a shiver tickled her back. She closed her eyes–lay there indeterminably long.

Light pierced her eyelids.

"Breaching."

The door slammed open. Boots shuffled in. Flashlight beams whizzed around like lightning strikes. Someone knelt by her, breathing. It smelled like spearmint. A cold finger touched her neck; she heard gentle clicking and rubbing of fabric.

"Are you conscious, ma'am?"

A low grunt. Her eyelids wouldn't hold open. They were made of lead.

"Aaron. One here."

"Room clear otherwise."

Fabric shifted. Static. "One alive. Albino, looks like. Yellow jumpsuit with the logo on."

A pause. Distortion spoke in return. "Extract to the atrium."

"Copy."

Rough hands found purchase on her. They hauled her into the air. Now her eyes peeled apart. She was staring up into the stubble of a man. His nose was large. She watched his breath wiggle hairs up his nostrils. "*Hh...*" She turned, saw Dewey where he lay. His skin was drained of color–so was his hair. Under his lids, she knew his eyes were albino red.

They weren't picking him up.

"*Wa... wa...*"

"Relax."

The ceiling opened up. She saw the cardinal painted on the wall. Consciousness came and went, interspersed with radio chatter. Her carrier wasn't interacting with it anymore. It sounded like the walkie was picking up disembodied voices. A group ran past. Her carrier spoke to his companions. She tried to count the voices.

"How the fuck does a place like this get built, anyway?"

"What do you mean?"

"Illegal shit slips through all the time. Earns me my paycheque."

Three voices. All men.

"It looks like a Scientology church in here."

"Well we caught these bastards anyhow–before they could drink the Kool-aid."

"Not Scientology."

"Huh?"

"You hear what happened in Waco? Something's going

on in this country."

A pause.

"What's with this girl, huh? Albino–looks like. But she doesn't look like one of 'em. Looks white… normal white, I mean. Was that other guy the same?"

"Yeah."

"Fucking nuthouse. Must've done experiments on them."

"Don't have to be African to be Albino."

"I thought you did."

"You see all that shit she threw up? Look at her. Looks like she's crying blood."

"Jesus."

Static. The walkie snapped, then rattled a few sentences.

"What the shit?"

"Huh? What did he say?"

"Gunfire. Third floor. Chris got hit."

"Fuck."

"Let's drop her quick."

Double doors swung open. Sunlight hit Roxanne's face. The darkness under her eyelids went pinkish-red. She opened them, saw the full-ceiling skylight. The room was brutalist, like the rest of the building, but decorated with tall ferns in planter boxes at each corner. Patterns were made with the sunlight by the plants' fan leaves.

She felt fabric under her. A cot. The man stepped away, and she saw the bold lettering on his jacket. *FBI*. Her head rolled to the side. Another cot. Another civilian. It was a woman–young. About nineteen. Glasses framed her eyes and freckled cheeks. She avoided eye contact.

Roxanne tried to speak. A cough came out instead of words. Sprinkles of the drug appeared on the girl's white cot. "I'm… sorry."

"Who are you?"

"What?"

Silence.

"Roxanne. Do you work here?"

"I'm the secretary."

"Oh. I'm, uh… I'm an operator."

"Hmm?"

"Do you… oh. I see."

"What?"

"They didn't tell you anything."

The girl frowned. She wore a dark pantsuit. Two pins held her collar down. Cardinals. "No, not really. I just file their documents with that box." A pause. "I don't think I've ever seen you here. You're uh… I…"

"I've been asleep in a back room for years."

Silence.

"You're not the secretary that was here when I was

awake."

The girl shifted. "They said she quit." Her eyes made a scan of the room. "Do you… know what's happening? I don't wanna go to jail."

"We won't go to jail."

An agent passed by. Another appeared, sat down on one of the concrete benches. It was a woman. Wrinkled face, tied blonde hair. Her plaid shirt was ruffled. One side was tucked and the other loose, like she couldn't make up her mind. Her face was accustomed to frowning. "What's your name, ma'am?"

"Roxanne."

"Last name?"

"Robbins."

"Alright." She pulled out a notepad. Wrote something down. "They said they found you in a back room in quite a state. Can you tell me what you were doing there, how you got there, and any other important details you feel I'd like to know."

"I… I'm an operator."

"What's that mean, ma'am?"

"They, uh… put me into the Red Runnel—that's uh… shit."

"Hmm?"

"I don't know how to explain this."

"Try your best."

"They were experimenting on me. Um… I'm the cousin of one of the scientists here. He, uh… He's dead now. They killed him. His name's Sonny Warren."

The pen scribbled lines.

"They, um…"

"Who's 'they', ma'am? You mean doct-"

"Otis Lang and Osian Molina."

"Alright."

"They developed a drug that can be used as a… a bioweapon, I guess. A neuroweapon. They wanted to sell it on the black market."

"What does it do?"

"What?"

"The drug?"

"It, uh… I guess it makes you invisible and lets you interact with… you can kill people without them knowing."

A smirk. The pen scribbled. "Alright. So Doctor Lang and Doctor Molina were experimenting on you, correct?"

"Yes."

"Alright."

"Can I ask why you're here?"

She looked up from the pad. "Why I'm here?"

"Yes."

"We're here because we received a tip there was money

laundering taking place." The pen was capped and slid through the notepad coil. "We seem to be finding a couple other things right off the bat."

"Like?"

"Well, human experimentation on yourself–provided that's the truth."

A pause. "This isn't a joke, ma'am."

The agent tilted her head to the side. "We're getting reports of shots fired on the third floor. Now I don't know what the other agents are finding in this place, but what it seems like to me is we've got potential organized crime activity–money laundering, sex trafficking, a front business to hide behind."

"I'm not a hooker."

"This building is pretty lavish. Lots of twists and turns and dead ends. Doors leading nowhere. At least that's what the other agents are radioing in. Can't find any labs or medication prepping, packaging, testing. Nothing."

BANG!

Roxanne almost leapt. She turned, saw three agents attempting to force the front door with a ram. A crowbar started chipping at the wood. There was metal behind it. There should have been a view of the yard–the sky.

"Are we in danger, ma'am?" The agent tapped her notepad.

"What's happening?"

"Do I need to spell it out?"

BANG! BANG! BANG! They gave up. Wood lay shattered across the ground. A steel shutter bore light scratching from the crowbar teeth.

"We have a search warrant. We weren't expecting this."

Roxanne crinkled her nose. "Who tipped you off to the money laundering?"

"It was anonymous." She roughly wedged the notepad into a pocket. "Miss Robbins. If you know what's happening, you need to tell me right now."

Her walkie spat. A voice came through clear enough. *"Found a DB. It's Chris. Santiago's gone. Counted six hostiles armed with AR's–patrolling the halls. Maybe we should call S.W.A.T. backup."*

Someone across the room answered. It was the same man who carried Roxanne. "Copy, Jill. Get back down here ASAP. I've already called them, over."

Fizzle. *"Copy, Lennon. I'm coming down. Hostiles were headed your way, by the look of it. Keep an eye out, over."*

"Miss Robbins?"

She shifted–looked back at the woman.

"Jesus… Are you gonna tell me anything?"

"I… I don't know…"

A sigh. The agent stood, brushed off her pants. "When

we get out of here, you'll be taken in for further questioning. *If* we get out of here." She leaned in. "But I'll let you in on a secret, missy. If I'm about to die–in the seconds before I bite it–and I know you could have saved my team… I'll blow your fucking brains across the wall as my last living action." A pause. "Mull that over in your head." Her boots thumped on the concrete. She became another moving body in the sea of moving bodies.

The leader–Lennon–spoke to her. He wore a frown–looked over at the two cots. She drifted off. He looked at Roxanne. Their eyes met, unconsciously.

A itch tickled her chest. She could hear her brain pumping in her skull.

SNAP! The bone of his eye socket shot out in little pieces.

"Motherfucker!" Someone yelled. Gunfire bit off the tail of his voice. Light flashed across the walls, like a firework had been set off.

Roxanne grabbed the secretary, dropped to the ground behind the planter box. "Are you oka–"

The girl's forehead was erupted.

"Oh.. oh my God." She couldn't look away.

Blood trickled down from the bullet wound, into her open eye.

Roxanne lay flat–went still. She tried to slow her

breathing. The gunfire was deafening. Pellets and dust fell across her back. From the corner of her eye, she saw a square opening in the wall. Fire spit from it–the barrel of a gun. There would be others like it, all around the room. She could tell by the noise.

Sudden silence.

Her head turned–as slow as she could make it. Bodies were strewn, covered in red. But she heard breathing. A table was flipped on its side, providing flimsy cover. The female agent sat behind, staring at the yellow-clad operator. In her eyes was something frightening.

"Fucking bitch." Her gun came up…

…and several shots rattled the table. It was only plastic–hardly a shield. The agent's upper torso was prodded with lead. Her gun clattered on the floor.

Click, click, click, click… click…

Each of the holes in the wall snapped closed.

SPIRITBOX

Her boot soles had thick treads—a front sole, and a two-inch heel. They left red prints on the concrete—the secretary's blood. She bent down to pick up one of the agent's pistols. Soaked in blood—she dropped it. There were others. She went for a second. The clip was empty. Various hard plastic crates were stacked around the atrium. Clasps snapped open, and lids lifted. There were vials inside—all empty. Each vial was printed with the cardinal logo.

No bullets.

She checked every gun. They were all empty. The bullets were wedged into the walls now—hundreds of them, fired in confusion. Her footsteps echoed. She came to one of the square outlines in the concrete, where she'd seen the gun barrels protruding. The wall was cold on her fingertip; she traced the seam, tried pushing it. It wouldn't move.

Thump...

A door.

She turned, looked up. There was a covered walkway around the perimeter of the atrium, on the second floor. Something moved along it–a man, with slicked blonde hair. He grabbed the rail–peered down at the massacre, then continued on. In his hand was a gun–but it didn't look like it fired bullets.

His footsteps rattled overhead, then a door slammed open and shut.

Silence returned.

"Coward." She went to the nearest door, opened it and passed through. The lights were off. Double doors at the end of the hall let in light through little reinforced windows. Large, white text was painted across both doors. *OFFICES*. She split the word in two, went through the doorway. A stairwell, echoing with footsteps. She started the ascent, and the footsteps grew faster.

He yelled: "Stop! Don't fucking follow me!"

No response came to her mind.

The door was still swinging closed when she got to it. *ADMINISTRATION*. She interrupted it, mid-motion– snapped it open again. He was sprinting down the hall. She matched his pace. He turned a corner, and she followed.

His office door shut. She knew it was locked before she tried the handle. "Otis Lang!"

Silence.

"It's Roxanne."

A pause. "I don't have anything to say to you." His voice was muffled, but audible.

She wrinkled her nose. "I'm here. Dewey unplugged me."

Silence.

"Did you hear me?"

"That dumb fuck. I should've gone in myself." He muttered something. "Can't find good help anymore. Why couldn't he just do his job?"

Something moved around inside. Two fogged glass windows flanked the door; she saw blobs of color and motion. "I'm gonna destroy the drug, Otis. The research, every vial. There's a S.W.A.T. team coming—the FBI called them in."

Silence.

"Otis?"

Thwip!

She frowned. "Hey!" She tried to force the door. "What are you doing?"

Silence.

"Shit." She stepped away. Her crimson eyes searched the half-light. Six doors, all shut. There were nameplates on every one, but she knew them all. The carpet muffled her boots. She marched to the last door on the left. *Jenny*

Brinkley. The knob turned without protest.

Jenny's office was neatly kept. Pictures of her family lined her desk on either side of a boxy computer. A calendar was thumb-tacked to the wall. *February 1998.* Her ID card and lanyard hung over the edge of her desk. It was looped around a pen cup. Pale fingers dug through the contents, moving aside the half-gnawed pencils and dried up pens.

Bobby pin.

She went back out into the hall, approached Lang's door. The pin slid into the keyhole and wormed its way through. She felt a click, and the knob turned. The room smelled of blood. Above the desk, on the wall, the grand image of the cardinal was spattered with it–an upward spray. Lang was slumped over his desk. Lacquered wood soaked up his blood.

"Oh my… God." She approached the corpse as if expecting it to reanimate. His hand was still clutching the odd firearm. It took little effort to pull it free. It was blocky– an oversized cassette tape, with many miles of copper wire wound up over and over inside the plastic shell. Something drew her attention. She looked up at the cardinal on the wall. It was stuck with a little metal pin. "What the…"

Her boot touched something. It was a cassette player. She bent down to retrieve it, and pressed the *Play* button. Otis Lang began to speak to her: *"I've been dodging calls from the FBI for a week now. Fucking secretary. I know she was speaking to Dewey quite a bit–let's hope she didn't put any funny ideas in his head. Should've killed that bitch as soon as I suspected something, but of course, I waited. Like an idiot. If they show up here... those pigs..."* She thought she heard sobbing. *"But the Redhoods, Otis. The Redhoods. The Redhoods will take care of them. Oh yeah, Osian, you fucking smartass! Your little Redhoods will save us! But you're a god-damn vegetable now, old coot. Your heart fucked ya! Where's the bravado now? ……. Maybe this is your punishment from God. Maybe you're right, huh? God is coming for you at last. Sister-fucking, murderous, little rat."* It stopped. She pressed the rewind button. It took a while to get to the start.

Someone closed a door.

Her heart skipped. The player had a clip, so she clipped it to her belt. She lifted the gun, made her way to the door. Nothing. The hall was still as death.

She left the body, and the room, for someone else to find.

—

A sigh. *"What do I say? This is for Osian–he wants me to keep an audio journal of my contributions to the project. Which right about now is damn close to jack-shit. Um...*

We're bringing in some guinea pigs to send into the Runnel. Osian calls them Operators. We'll see what they find in there–this is our first time exposing actual people to the drug."

Roxanne turned a corner, found another stretch of hallway. To the right were floor-to-ceiling glass windows. A conference room, with the blinds up. The chairs around the table inside were neatly tucked. Someone had drawn on a whiteboard, then crudely erased it. *Ex...per...nts Un...tak...n.*

The tape player droned on. *"He's been spending more time in the basement. I don't even know what he's doing down there–he doesn't let anyone see. Keeps the basement locked. We had to move all our important shit from down there up to the sixth floor. I went down there once to see–my card didn't work on the scanner. He's probably got it set to accept his and no one else's. Whatever. I never used to go down anyway. Just a bunch of pipes carrying our shit water."*

Silence. The tape still turned. After a moment, the voice came back. *"Haven't made an entry in months."*

She pressed the elevator button. The faded plastic lit up, and the room hummed. She thought she heard distant gunfire.

"We uh... sent six operators in. They say the world is

gray in there, except for the color red. They're calling it the Red Runnel now. Uh... Osian says it's something to do with the rods and cones or cones and rods or whatever in our eyes. Light only reflects off of red objects yadda-yadda. I wasn't paying attention, to be honest."

The doors slid open. She stepped through.

"Um... Yeah, we got two new operators last week. Robbins and Warren. They're related—cousins, I think. Girl's kinda hot, so that gives me something to stare at aside from test tubes and the back of Molina's bald head."

She frowned.

"Warren's an interesting one. Smart fucker. He's young, though. Around thirty. Apparently they lived in some bumfuck village in Romania; their family was noble, so they had some big mansion or castle or some shit. Both of 'em are pale as all hell—maybe they're vampires."

Gravity yanked on the elevator as it slowed. The doors pulled apart to bear a lightless hallway. She stuck her head out—looked left, then right. Only one door at the far end was illuminated. It stuck out like a beacon.

"Osian's having Warren work with him in the lab. He helped the old coot solve some kind of problem he's been working on for months. Guess I'll be out of a job in a little bit." A laugh. It was almost forced. The tape went quiet again.

She reached down to stop it. A carpet muffled her boots–made her approach silent. The door had a fogged glass window; writing was carefully painted on. *Doctor Osian Molina, M.D., D.V.M., Psy.D.* The knob was cold. It turned–clicked–and the door swung.

He sat in a wheelchair by the window. There were FBI vehicles across the courtyard–a S.W.A.T. truck just pulling in. She couldn't see his face. "Wh-wh-who is-s-s it?"

A pause. "Roxanne."

The wheelchair turned. Half his face seemed melted; the other half was smiling. "W-w-w-well then. W-w-what a surp-pr-p-prise." His head gently shook–an uncontrollable motion. "I n-n-never expected to s-s-s-see you ag-g-again."

Her fingers found a better grip on the gun. "A mite got you."

"Unf-f-fortunately."

A box of cigars sat open on his desk. Tall ferns shrouded his mustard wallpaper. She scanned his bookshelves–hundreds of spines stared back. They seemed to her like trophies–like the mounted heads of a game hunter. All of them dead–gone through, and placed there to give ambiance to the room.

"Y-y-you ha-ha-have Otis' g-g-g-gun."

She looked down at it.

"He m-m-m-made that, you know." Another smile. "One

of h-h-his only acc-cc-cc-accomplishments. Used to t-t-tinker in the g-garage with his father. He w-w-was a smart man, e-ev-v-ven if he didn't k-know it."

"I'm gonna destroy all your research." She paused. "I wanted you to know that."

"Bef-f-fore you sh-sh-shot me?"

Silence.

"Do y-y-y-you see that?" A finger touched the window. "Th-th-they're c-c-coming for me. B-b-but my R-r-r-redhoods are wait-t-ting. Th-they'll p-p-protect me with their lives. Th-th-that is devotion."

She lifted the gun.

"I sh-sh-shouldn't h-h-have trusted B-b-becker. Your c-c-cousin preys up-up-upon weak minds."

BANG!

There was no time to turn around. An arm wrapped around her neck, and she felt a sharp pain. A glance revealed some kind of needle. There were flashes of red, then she was laid on the ground. The wheelchair rolled past, guided by a red-clad man.

"Sw-w-w-weet r-r-r-remembr-r-rance, Rox-x-x-anne."

Her eyelids forced themselves shut.

HOME

Rain rattled the window panes.

The room smelled like horses and scented candles. She opened her eyes. Four wooden walls closed her in, and wooden rafters ran above her head. Dried herbs hung from them by string—some had little flowers. Her feet slid off the bed—touched the ground. The yellow boots were gone—so was the jumpsuit. She ran her hands along her pantleg—jeans. The skin of her hand was pale, but not colorless. "What is this?"

She went to the front window. Sunset; it made the glass into amber. Mist wrapped a distant mountain range—snaked through the trees around the village.

"Jesus." Her reflection caught her eye—an eye of blue, not albino red. "What did… he do to me?" She checked her neck, felt a little wound—a needle prick.

A click. The door handle turned flimsily; she pushed it open. The air reeked of smoke.

"*Bună seara dragă.*"

She spun in place. It was an old woman, her skirts caked in mud. Her face was familiar. "*Bună seara.*" The words came back to her. "*Ce... ce an este?*"

A laugh. A wide smile split the wrinkled visage. "*Suntem în 1987, dragă.*" Her rough hands worked to straighten her shirt. Gray hair was bound in a kerchief. "*Unde este mama ta? Du-te acasă la ea.*"

"I..."

Her slippers pushed mud. A slow, hobbling pace took her down the road.

Roxanne looked around. A farmer across the way cut lucerne with a scythe. His pigs dug their snouts into the muck, carving trails. She followed the road with her eyes. It led where she expected it to. A mansion sat atop the hillock, overwatching the village. Lights were on in the windows.

She started walking.

CASA ROBESCU. Wind and rain had battered the wooden sign. A pointing hand was inked onto the chipping boards. Something hung by a string. It laid itself flat in her palm as she reached up, and she flipped it over and back again. A crucifix, with Christ cast in metal. On the back, etched in, read: *Se vor încolăci.* She read it–muttered to herself. "They will cower..."

It found its way into her pocket.

The door was locked. Her father's face was carved in wood. It stared down at her as she tried the handle. Her mother, on the door beside him, gazed into the interminable. A rusting lantern swung overhead with the coaxes of the wind. Mist from the forest was settling over the village; she could barely see out the front gate.

"Damn it." She wrinkled her nose. A moment's walk brought her to the side of the house, where a tree stump protruded from the grass. There was a stone plaque affixed to it. She knew what it said, but read anyway.

Odihnească-se în pace.

Acest copac i-a luat viața.

Cadavrul lui este mormântul ei.

She squinted. Someone had carved English below.

Rest in peace.

This tree took her life.

Its corpse is her tomb.

Her finger ran over the letters. They were sloppy—unlike the carefully etched Romanian. The finger came to rest on a familiar protrusion, pressed down, and ejected a key. It was cold metal—antique. As she passed back along the house, one of the windows lost its light, and another sparked up. She stopped. Waited. A cart rolled past the front gate, hauling passengers. They gawked at the mansion.

She continued. A cattle prod lay against the foundation. It was heavy in her hand. She took it anyway. Her mother's wooden visage looked down in shame; she grasped the mouth and pulled down, revealing a keyhole between the lips. She choked her mother with the key, twisted, and felt a click. A gentle push opened the door–let loose a gust of stagnance.

"*Tată?*" She called out into the dark foyer. "*Eşti aici?*"

Silence.

A click. The door shut behind her, and she locked it. A lamp on a squat chest of drawers fizzled to life when she tugged its cord. Family photos were framed behind dusty glass. She smiled–stared down at an image of herself with a less-formed face, dressed in a school uniform.

"Roxana." His face hung in the darkness. His clothes were midnight black.

She turned. "Aaron?"

His accent was plain and unplaceable. "Your father is ill, Roxana."

"What?"

"Go to him. He's in his room." A pause. "I won't ask where you were."

The picture frame returned to its place, but face down.

She kept the cattle prod, climbed the stairs. Aaron's pale face hung in the shadows. It followed her as she passed. There was no warmth coming from his figure–like he was a corpse. He said: "I must return to your father's accounting." But he didn't move.

They locked eyes. She took a step, and another. "Aaron?"

"Yes, Roxana?"

Silence.

"What day is it?"

"The fifth of September."

Silence.

Her fingers adjusted on the prod. "Nineteen eighty seven?"

"Yes, Roxana."

"Is my father shipping me to America?"

Silence.

Her shoes thumped on the carpet. A hallway was lit by bulbs enclosed in gaslamp housings. Paintings hung in every space where there wasn't a window or door. She glanced over her shoulder. Aaron was gone.

She sighed–wavering–continued down the hall. The door at the far end was ajar, letting light spill into shadow. She drifted the distance, felt her head spinning. The hinges screamed when she pushed the door–it sounded human. Her father sat in a chair by the window, soaking in the orange sunset. There was a faint movement of his head–a voice that filled the room. "Roxana. *Vino aici.*"

"How did you know I was here?

"*Nu vorbi american!*"

"But you're sending me there. Why shouldn't I speak it?"

Silence.

"The house is rotting."

Now her father acquiesced. His English was butchered. "Aaron is lazy. He can't fix. Dumb Englishman."

She smiled.

"Come here, *dragă*. Let me see you."

The walk towards the chair seemed to chase her soul away. She knelt by him and examined the faint vestige of her father. "Why are you sending me away?"

He groaned. "I am dead."

"Dying."

"Ah… yes. Speak like them already." He touched her hand. "For you, there is nothing here. America is for the young. This country is old." A frown. "*Acolo vei trăi o viață mai bună.*"

A tear fell onto the velvet chair. "But it's not, *tată*. My life is not good there… why… If you knew what they would do to me…" Her head came to rest on his hand.

"Come now." His free hand stroked her dark hair. "My daughter is strong."

For a time, they sat in silence. The sunset fled behind the mist-swept mountains.

"Your heart is good," he said. "Your cousin is good. Listen. He is smart boy."

No response. She felt sleep's luring.

"Love you."

She woke in the morning with the sun warming her face. Her cheek was pressed against the velvet armrest. She looked around the room, more decrepit in the sunlight. Her father was gone.

—

A statue loomed over the foyer from the staircase landing. It was a robed man clutching a sickle in one hand, and a heart in the other. The heart was a cow's, she'd been told, but it looked far too human. She moved through the rays of sunshine—dust filled and tepid on her skin. The air still reeked of smoke, both inside and out. She grabbed the front door handle, turned. It stuck. She rattled it—dust fell over her. A step back, and a look around the room. "I need to leave." Silence. "Aaron!"

No answer.

Her neck felt cold to the touch. The needle hole was still there–swollen now. A bump, like a hive. "What did he put in me?" She rubbed her neck. "Shit."

All life seemed to have fled the house. No matter which room she entered, or door she opened, every one was empty. She tapped the cattle prod on the carpet as she walked. It sent a vibration through the floorboards. She wrinkled her nose, pushed aside her bangs.

She stopped.

"Oh." The stairs thumped and creaked under her weight. She hurried to the nearest window, prod in hand. "Sorry Aaron. If you're even here."

THWACK! The window rattled. She frowned. *THWACK... CRACK...*

"Are you..." Her palm met the glass. She felt around. Not a scratch. "Alright." She almost tripped on the carpet walking backward. A few steps. A few more. Her arm extended, then hurled.

BANG!

The prod clattered off, struck the floorboards. She bent down to pick it up.

"Having trouble, miss?"

She spun in place. "I..." She gaped back at herself in the reflection of a clock face. A neck held it aloft, then a body–dressed in an ornate military coat.

The clock lifted his hands. "Do not fear me, *dragă*. Come closer and speak with me. I may have something which can *ajuta la problema ta.* Yes?"

She didn't move.

"I am merely a jovial clock, *dragă*."

"I've never seen a talking clock." She found a two-handed grip on the prod.

The clock hands spun thrice over. "I appear for those who are lost, *dragă*. To tell them that they have time to waste, yes? *Timpul merge mereu înainte.*" A thin hand beckoned eagerly. "Come here, *dragă*."

She obeyed, warily.

"See? I am harmless." He reached up to pluck a latch, and the glass covering his clock-face swung open. "You are late, you see. Time is running thin."

"What do you mean?"

"Molina attempts escape, of course. This drug he has forced into you works to keep you... sleeping. There is ample time for him to flee, yes?"

"I... I don't... How do I wake up?"

"Leave the village, of course. But that is *mai uşor de zis decât de făcut*." He slammed shut the glass cover. "Perhaps I might gift something to you which can start you upon this quest. There is much yet to do once you awaken."

"Give it to me."

"Ah, patience, *dragă. Aminteşte-ţi manierele tale.* What would your father think of such behavior?" The hands spun around again. "But you are a pretty girl, and so I'll give it to you for free, yes?" Out from his coat came a small, metal badge. It bore the likeness of the macabre statue. "You know its use, yes?"

"Yes."

"Good." He took her hand, opened the fingers, and placed the badge. "And another deal, I'll make with you. Bring me what awaits, and I shall open the front door."

Silence.

"Why not open it now?"

"I cannot, you see."

"Why?"

"You are a curious girl, *dragă.* Perhaps I shall tell you once you retrieve my bauble."

The prod tapped the ground.

"And do not think of smashing such a beautiful clock. Then you'll be trapped here forever, yes? *Putreind cu casa.*"

She looked down at the badge. "Fine." It slipped into her pocket. "What's the clock's name? Does he have one?"

"Knoxy," said the clock. "Such a pretty asks my name! How sweet the morning is!"

STRIGOI

Claws tapped against the window.

She gasped. A dog pressed its nose to the glass; its breath was made fog. There was something wrong with its eyes. It pushed off, patted away.

The hallway lamp flickered.

She stood before a bookcase, scanning the spines. They were all in Romanian. Between the middle row was pressed a wooden block–a relief cut intricately into its outward face by hand. She fit the badge–pressed it firmly.

Thunk...

The bookshelf swung open. She grabbed it–pulled to make it open faster. Then she entered the hidden space, knowing to expect a sudden plunge into darkness. A staircase, with steps of hewn stone. Her footsteps ricocheted off the close walls–the low ceiling. The air was thin.

Little frames were nailed to the cobblestone walls. She squinted. They were daguerrotypes–hardly visible in the poor light. In one, an old woman sat with her arm resting on a small table. Her head was bound in a bonnet. A man stood with his scythe in the next, hair disheveled. Light from the entryway glinted in the polished silver faces.

At the bottom of the stairs was a short room—opposing walls on the left and right were hidden behind bottle racks. She knew the alcohol. *Țuică*. Wires ran along the ceiling from a dirty bulb—ended at a switch screwed into the stone. She flicked it, blinked as the bulb fizzled. It revealed a small table. Papers were strewn across it, along with another framed daguerrotype. It drew her eye. Her heart skipped.

The creature photographed had rotted skin, dark as molasses. Sunken eyes stared off into nothing. Crooked fangs protruded from a small, pursed mouth. The ears were pointed, like a lynx, with tufts of hair sticking up. She grabbed the image and flipped it over, then brushed her fingers across her jeans. The first paper was neatly scribed— she slid it closer.

I placed Sebastian's boy on the whitest horse we have. The lad had to wear his father's wedding suit. He looked funny, I admit, swallowed by that white jacket. Nigh on the whole town followed me as I led the horse to the cemetery. Then I let it walk.

It stopped after six graves. They dug up the coffin, and had no need to pry the nails from the lid. They wished me to capture it with my camera—the thing they pulled from there. I did so, then destroyed the camera and burned it. It is the devil, and to think it was loose here. It laid hands upon that girl. The fangs—rotted and unholy—piercing her white flesh. God has abandoned us here. Satan has a hold upon this village, letting his ilk ravage us.

They cut the head from its body, and buried it face down. If it wakes again, it shall tunnel back to Hell.

There was a date beneath. *August 1854.*

"Jesus." She left the table.

Something moaned.

She gripped the prod and spun around. In the corner of the room, just out of the light, something pulsated. Liquid had pooled underneath—it started running through the grooves of the cobblestone. It was dark and opaque. Something overcame her. She lifted the prod—reached out with it. The end touched the mass, and the pool widened. Blackness wept from every crease and orifice.

"God… seriously…"

Thoop… The flesh peeled back to reveal a pearl. It sparkled, even in shadow. With the end of the prod, she plucked it free, and it rolled across the ground. She chased it, dropping to her knees. It was trapped under her hands. She stood, opened her fingers. It sat in her palm. "Bauble. Alright. Maybe."

Her foot was yanked.

She fell on her shoulder, dropping the pearl. A writhing tentacle emitted from the mass had wrapped her ankle. The prod had fallen to the side–she reached for it... But it was too far away. The flesh was warm. It enveloped her leg, then her other–her torso, arms. Once her head was swallowed, it sealed itself, and continued to pulsate quietly in the corner of the room.

—

She was bound in mire.

Ropey tar restricted her arms. Her legs were untied, however. She got to a seated position, then stood. Everything around her was dark and wet. The walls were black flesh–gyrating. "What…" Her shoe tried for footing; there was no ground–only the rounded bottom of this living flesh sack. Many times, she stumbled and fell. Her clothes were stained black; her face was splotched with it–hair stuck with it. There were tunnels, barely wide enough to fit through. Arteries. She found one, stepped in, and listened as the flesh groaned.

It was a slide–a flesh slide. She sat and pushed off. The ride was slow; she couldn't sit upright–the slide would move under her. A brake–she rolled forward. Her constricted arms tried to break free. She tumbled into an open cavern, landed face-down. A groan, then she tried to roll onto her back. Her eyes searched wildly. Something was keeping the various cavities lit–without an obvious source. She could see right across–and the thing sitting there, on an outcropping of flesh.

It looked as if a Great Dane and a man had made some kind of bestial offspring. Flesh was sealed over the space for its mouth. Large eyes never blinked.

Ssip... k...k...k...k...k...

It stood. The limbs extended fully.

Roxanne writhed, trying to break her bondage. "Shit!... Come o-o-o-o-n!" She was running out of breath. She rolled to the side, gasped.

There was no floor under her.

SMACK!

The final dregs of breath were forced out of her lungs. She sucked in the stale air.

The lanky thing peered over the ledge she'd fallen off of. It clicked–like a bat. Then it turned away and vanished. Once it stopped clicking, it was swallowed sonically by the squirming flesh.

"Son-of-a-bitch." She held back tears. A push from her leg rolled her onto her side.

She shrieked–cut it off quick.

Another of the lanky things was half-absorbed by the blackness. The ground was growing over its corpse. It was like a dead spider, limbs seized in morbid configurations. Hands. With claws.

A great effort got her to her feet. She approached, pressed herself up to the hand–the claw. It snapped the black ropes like blades of grass. Her hand was free, then her other. She wriggled out of the rest, letting it fall to the ground. "Thanks, I guess." She was about to walk away. Stopped, turned around. She grabbed one of the fingers, bent it awkwardly, using it to saw off the adjacent one. There was no blood. It popped free, and she examined her new tool. It was pale; the nail was like a cat's. Curved, for hooking and tearing. She started walking, while trying to find the best way to grip it.

Dead end.

She looked up, down, and behind. There were no tunnels or arteries to slip through.

Thump… Thump…

The flesh above her moaned, pulsated. It was raw–a wound, festering and crawling. An ulcer of shadow, leaking off-white cream. *"Call the doctor… call the doctor… call the doctor… CALL THE DOCTOR…"* It was a rasping whisper, emanated from somewhere inside the gash. *"Tatăl e pe moarte… Tatăl e pe moarte… Tatăl e pe moarte… Tatăl e pe moarte…"*

She dug the claw into the fleshy wall. It sawed roughly, carving a jagged opening. Light slipped in, doing little against the dark. She rammed her hand in, felt around. Air. Her shoulders barely fit lengthwise. Her weight tore the cut a little more. She slumped out like a fish, cracking her head on the floorboards. A gasp–she sucked in the stale basement air. Her clothing stuck to the ground. She turned, saw the lump of flesh in the corner; it had stopped moving–deflated. "Fuck. What the fuck?"

The pearl still sat there, caught in a crack between the floorboards. She picked it up. A sigh. She paused to take a breath. The stairs creaked and complained under the weight of her shoes. Once she was at the summit, she pulled the badge from its slot in the bookshelf and let the heavy thing groan shut. A click. Then silence.

—

"The pretty is fair and wise to hold up her end. Let me see it. *Asa o frumusete.*" The clock took the pearl delicately between two fingers, held it up to the light. "Just as I remember it, *dragă.*"

"Now let me out… please."

The clock face popped open. Deft hands slotted the pearl

into the empty divet just beneath the twelfth hour. The face swung shut again. "Yes, of course. Though it saddens me to see the pretty go." A key danced soundlessly between his fingers. It came to rest in his palm, which he opened to her.

She took the key, recognized her father's face engraved intricately into the metal.

"There are wicked things in the village at nighttime, *dragă*. That is why I could not let you leave."

A frown. "What?"

"*Scuza-ma*, for it was impossible to let you die in so nasty a fashion. You carry a piece which can protect you from them, yet it is a piece incomplete–and therefore useless." The clock seemed to display hesitancy. The face popped open again, and a quick finger spun both hands around until they flanked the inset pearl. *Pop*... The pearl snapped open–it wasn't a pearl at all. It was a container– holding a red jewel no larger than a pebble. "This is the soul of Christ, *dragă*. And as they say, the eyes are the window." He held open his hand and the jewel popped free. Now he opened his other hand, and waited.

She stared, blinked. From her pocket came the crucifix necklace. She noticed now that Christ's face was missing–an empty divet.

The clock took the necklace and placed the jewel into the hole. It fit perfectly. "Now it is usable."

"Usable?"

"They will cower, *dragă*. When they see the face of Christ."

A pause. "Who will?"

"The villagers. If they come close, draw this and hold it aloft." He demonstrated. "*Strigoii sunt diavoli,* yes?"

"Oh…" She took back the necklace.

"Do not fear them, *dragă*. They are given power by your fear." The clock hands spun. "Now the pretty must go, before time is up."

"Thank you."

The clock shuddered. "It is my pleasure to assist, *dragă*. Your thanks is worth a thousand polished gears, yes?"

She smiled. "I know this is all in my head. But I can't figure out where you came from."

"A mystery to be sure. I was always willing to listen."

The smile was sapped away. She walked towards the door, gripped the handle. When she glanced over her shoulder, he was gone. In his place stood a tall grandfather clock. It's pendulum was still. Small metal letters were bolted to the varnished wood, just below the face. A brand name. *Knoxy.*

She inserted the key, turned, and the front door unlocked.

THE BODY

A gramophone was half buried in the dirt. It played Chopin's *Nocturne in F Minor* through a curtain of static. And a voice.

"And he said unto them, with desire I have desired to eat this passover with you before I suffer. For I say unto you, I will not any more eat thereof, until it be fulfilled in the kingdom of God."

She shut the door behind herself. The wooden jaw of her mother's carving snapped shut with the latch. The mist had rolled in from the forests; it settled over the yard and hid the village from her. Dogs bayed and howled from somewhere unseen. Her feet crushed fallen leaves. The gramophone spit and crackled as she approached.

"And he took bread, and gave thanks, and broke it, and gave unto them, saying, This is my body which is given for you: this do in remembrance of me."

The crucifix hung from her clenched fist. She went to the front gate—peered through the iron bars at the shrouded road.

Phantom lights hung in the mist, where the village houses lay. She pushed, and the hinges screamed.

"Likewise also the cup after supper, saying, this cup is the new testament in my blood, which is shed for you."

The air was close. She could hear her own breathing in her head. The crucifix clicked gently. It felt almost warm in her grip.

Footsteps.

A dark silhouette took form–coming up the road.

She went silent.

Something moved behind her, back toward the house. It was a ragged dog, eyes pearls of black. It snapped its jaws.

"But, behold, the hand of him that betrayeth me is with me on the table."

She felt breath on her face.

"Vino aici, scumpo."

Cold fingers wrapped around her neck. They tried to pull her near. She turned and gaped into the face of death. Its eyes were sunken, skin sallow and rotted. Fangs extruded from a pursed mouth, dripping venom.

Her hand came up, bearing the crucifix.

The beast hissed and spat, then it leapt into the air and tumbled away, becoming enveloped in shadow and cloth, which turned to thin flesh. A bat–big as an eagle. It flitted off into the mist.

"Shit."

Now the dog. It lunged. Mid-air, its canine face became human.

She stepped aside, then sprinted for the house. It followed—now half man: human hands and canine legs.

She tried the door. It wouldn't open. She pried her mother's lips apart, but she didn't have the key anymore. A glance over her shoulder—she expected to see teeth closing over her.

"*And the Lord said, Simon, Simon, behold, Satan hath desired to have you, that he may sift you as wheat.*"

It lay there, human eyes wide as saucers. The fingers clutched the grass—unclutched, dug. Its body was still canine—as were its champing teeth. "*Nu te ascunde în spatele lui Dumnezeu.*" A dark growl. The fangs extruded, long as knives.

"*And he said unto him, Lord, I am ready to go with thee, both into prison, and to death.*"

It began to writhe. Blood ran in rivulets down its cheeks. The fangs snapped. "*Vino la mine!*"

"Don't like the music?" She stood. The string of the necklace was interlaced with her clutched fingers. She lifted it where the beast could see.

The sound it made was beyond vile. A chugging scream— cut off as it rolled away and padded out to the road. When it turned back, it had the face of a dog again. Its eyeshine stood out amidst the darkness. In a moment, it was gone.

A breath. She crept towards the gate. Stopped.

Silence.

Somewhere, a bird trilled.

She stepped onto the road. "*Pa, tată.*" She walked, fast, ignoring her surroundings. The road was quiet. It descended the hill into the village; at its end, she saw the looming forms of houses beginning to appear. The church tower was a black spike. Its bell chimed in the quiet–sonorous.

Crack... A door shut–she watched it happen. Beside it was a black window; she felt something watching through it.

The road ran down the center of the village. She stepped onto the grass, crept along the side of a house. Behind it was an assortment of rusted tools half buried in the dirt. Two wooden trunks supported a corrugated metal sheet; water dripped off into the mud. It was meant to shield a stack of firewood from the rain. Something else was soaking it all, however.

She inched towards it–a body, guts pulled out through a split open torso. A cloud of black flies scented rot. It was old–the skin was starting to darken and shrink over the remainder of the skeleton. She plugged her nose. "What the... fuck."

Splashing. It took her a moment to recognize it. She

ducked behind a busted crate. And waited.

"*Te miros.*"

A voice. It sounded like decay.

"*Vino la mine.*" The thing revealed itself from around the edge of the wall. Pointed ears. Long, scraggly hair hung damp in the wet air. It hissed, like an angry cat–sprayed venom. "*Piele dulce. Sânge dulce.*"

She held her breath.

It dragged its feet. She listened to its movement–tracked it in her head. Then she thought of something.

The crucifix was lifted over the edge of the crate. She felt pain in her hand, dropped the necklace. Blood was crawling out of three marks clawed across her fingers.

But the thing was screaming.

She looked over the crate, saw it waving around a burning hand. It tried to gnaw at its wrist. It tripped over a rake, hit the mud–writhed and twisted.

With her other hand, she picked up the necklace. She bared it to the creature. It screamed louder. She let the crucifix touch the decomposing flesh, and it set fire to it. Now the thing was consumed in a ball of flame.

Footsteps. Many of them.

She spun a circle, saw nothing. But the steps were closing in. There could have been hundreds. She sprinted, past the defiled stack of firewood and the burning monster.

Amongst the cacophony of sound, she heard violent voices.

"*Vreau să gust din ea!*"

"*E frumoasă!*"

"*Mănâncă-o! Mănâncă-o! Mănâncă-o!*"

A hand grabbed at her. It snapped away the necklace, and she heard animalistic shrieks–saw the glow of flame. "No!"

The mud tried to suck at her shoes. She saw the crooked fence posts that marked the entrance to the village.

Claws dug into her back

She screamed–hit the ground. They crawled on top of her, slashing and biting. Fangs sunk into her neck, and she felt blood being drawn. She wept and screamed.

And after what seemed like hours of pain, she died.

THE DOLLMAKER

And woke.

On the floor of Osian Molina's office. Rain was striking the window panes. She sat up, reached up to feel her neck. The inflammation was gone; it took a second to feel the hole. There was something shiny next to her on the ground. A little pen–metal, with a tuft of red sticking out the end. The opposing end was a stubby needle. It was coated in blood.

She picked it up. Small black letters were printed on the metal. *Tranq Pen – Carisoprodol.* She drowsily threw it across the room. "Shit."

The building shook.

She stumbled to the window–leaned against the sill with both hands. There was a S.W.A.T. truck, and men in kevlar scattered across the front yard. To the left, and down, she saw a tank. A long metal arm was attached, and now halfway stuck through the building's wall. Gas was leaking from the puncture.

"You damn… fucking idiots." She wrinkled her nose. "I'm not done yet."

Flashes of her dream spun behind her eyes. It had been the same dream. Again.

Her yellow boots clunked and shuffled–drunken. She got to her knees, put her cheek against the linoleum. Nothing behind the flower pot. A shift. Nothing behind the doctor's Dewbox. Finally, she checked under his desk. It was there, untouched. "Smart doctor you are." Her hand delved into the darkness, felt the metal, pulled it into the light. The gun was still loaded.

The door crept open. She peered into the hall. Nothing. She slipped out, and into the adjacent elevator. "Wha…" No buttons. Only a keyhole. "Come on, you… sneaky bastard." Back into the office. A minute's search was fruitless. Every drawer in the polished wooden desk was empty. No paper, no paperclips, no junk. The room had been stripped.

The large ferns toppled–spilled onto the hardwood. Dirt went everywhere. She looked behind–nothing but a round, discolored mark on the boards. She yanked drawers out and spun them in her hands, checking all sides. Nothing. She threw them into a pile. A grunt. All her weight fought against the heft of the desk.

SNAP! The desktop split. She pushed, broke off a jagged hunk of varnished wood. "Huh."

It joined the drawers in their pile.

She sat on the unbroken side, hunched over. The gun flitted between her left hand, and her right. She scanned briefly. Clouds parted, allowing a ray of sunlight through the rain. It washed across the far back wall, and the painting that hung there. Osian Molina was framed beside a woman. She was dark–hair black and eyes sunken into shadow.

Roxanne lifted the gun–aimed down the sights. Considered.

Thwip!

Out of the barrel came a metal pin–faster than a blink. It struck the likeness of the doctor–under his left eye… and went clean through.

She frowned.

The desk croaked as she got off. Her heels echoed in the emptied out office. The painting was incredibly detailed; she could see the sadness in the woman's face. She felt the canvas with her fingers. It bowed inward. The frame lifted easily off its nail, and she set it down on the floor. There was a recess behind–and a key hanging from a small metal hook.

And a folded paper.

She took it, peeled it apart. Spidery litters were scribbled messily across the off-white page. *I lost my eye today. He took it from me, and gave me a glass replacement. It hurts. I think it's too big. But he won't let me take it out. My socket will become infected if I do, he says. He's made me so pretty. When I see myself in the mirror, I can't help but gasp. I want to cry, but my eyes won't let me. I'm beautiful. I love him. I love him. I love him. I love him. With all my heart and soul. I love my doctor.*

She replaced it. "What the hell?"

The key jingled as she plucked it off. She hurried back to the elevator and tried it. It slotted in perfectly–twisted and clicked. The doors shut, and the big box shook lethargically. Her fingers fidgeted on the pistol grip. There was shooting on one of the floors that passed by. Muted gunshots faded in, and out–no more than a second. A red light blinked along an arched display of bulbs. Beneath each was a floor number. It reached the end: *B*. The doors opened–metal lips. On the other side was a black curtain. Darkness.

She stepped out, bathed in red glow. There was a lightswitch. It took some force to flick it.

Industrial-style lamps buzzed and spat.

The walls were white panels. There was a cage–alone in the middle of the room. Something fleshy moved inside.

Her footsteps drew its attention.

"No-o-o-o-o… No more… No-o-o-o-o-o-o-o mo-o-o-o-o-ore." It paused. "Kill me. Kill me-e-e-e-e."

She approached. She had to bend down to peer through the bars. Her crimson eyes searched for a recognizable shape.

"Kill me. Kill me. Kill me kil me mkil me kill em kil lmemlkillke mkill killme KILL ME!" The man was butchered–stitched around his joints. Every limb was a separate skin tone. Some of the stitches were starting to come apart.

"What's your name?"

"Kill me. Kill me. Kill me."

"Who… did this to you?"

"Kill me. Kill me. Kill me."

"Are you hearing me?"

"Kill me. Kill me. KILL ME!"

She lifted the gun. *Thwip!*

Silence.

Her eyes lingered on the corpse. "Jesus."

There was a single door. It was black. She went to it, tried the handle. It opened, but the wave of odor halted her before she stepped through. Decay, and human waste. It made her want to gag. "Mother of God. What the fuck…" More cages. And gurneys. Insects crawled up and down the corners of the walls. She found the light switch, and wished immediately that she hadn't.

Lying on each gurney was a female corpse, stripped of clothing. Blank faces gaped up at the ceiling. A rolling metal table to the side was covered in prosthetic eyeballs–every color. Roxanne approached and looked down at the faces. Something tugged hard at her chest, making her want to scream.

There was a workbench—metal, covered in dried blood and viscera. A note was pinned to the wall above it.

Number 1 : Hair correct, face correct, body correct. Eyes wrong, skin wrong.

Number 2 : Eyes correct, face correct, skin correct. Hair wrong, body wrong.

Number 3: Eyes correct. Hair wrong, face wrong, body wrong, skin wrong.

She stepped away, turned to the cages. They were occupied. Human forms moaned and moved faintly. Each one was malformed. A man with no arms, a man with four arms, a woman with no lips or nose, a child with no legs.

"Fuck…" Roxanne passed all of them. There was a door at the end of the room. She burst through and shut it. A dim hall. Light spilled through a door at the end; shadows moved across the gap between the door and the frame. She gripped the gun with both hands, took a step…

"Lady… lady…"

…stopped. She turned around, pressed her ear up to the door.

"Come back. I have to speak. Speak to you. Lady… lady…"

The handle was cold. She was hit with the stench again. She peered through into the chamber. It scanned over the cages–the gently moving lumps of flesh. One of them, in the middle, wasn't moving. It was a man, sitting bolt upright–eyes wide and staring at the door. "Come. Lady… lady… come here. Quick…"

She slipped through.

"Yes. yes. yes… come." He had no hands. Crusting bandages were wound over every inch of his body. A mummy. "Your footsteps are so light. Lady steps."

"Excuse me?"

"What are you doing down here? This is our little home. We've had no guests… ever. Never."

She wrinkled her nose. "Did… Osian Molina do this to you? The doctor?"

"Yes, yes, yes. The doctor. The doctor. Mad doctor. But we love him. He is our only love." A smile formed between the bandages. Gums were shrunken back from rotting, nearly canine teeth. "Who are you lady? Lady… lady…"

A pause. "I'm gonna kill the doctor."

"NO! DON'T YOU FUCKING DARE!" He tried to stand, but his brittle form fought him. His jaws parted–a warped scream crawled out. "He made me beautiful! Beautiful! Beautiful! I love him. Love him. Love him. DON'T FUCKING TOUCH HIM OR I'LL CUT OFF

YOUR SKIN AND EAT YOUR MUSCLES AND BONES AND GRIND YOUR SKULL."

The gun found a spot between the mummy's eyes.

"He's not in the next room. No. He's not in the next room. Cain will bend you over and have his way. He'll rape you and cut off your head and eat your spine! CAIN WILL EAT YOUR SPINE! LIKE A FISH SPINE! CRUNCHY AND NUTRITIOUS!"

"Who's Cain?"

"Captain, captain, captain, captain. Do you like being hurt lady? He'll hurt you."

Silence.

"Is that a gun? Gun? Gun? Gun? SHOOT ME? DON'T DO IT! THE DOCTOR WANTS TO HAVE HIS WAY WITH ME. HE'S NOT DONE. NO, HE'S NOT DONE WITH ME. I WANT HIM TO HURT ME MORE. HU-

A pin punctured the bandages, then came out the other side of the skull. The mummy slumped over and went still.

She left him—as fast as possible. The door shut on the room of cages. She didn't open it again. The shadows at the end of the hall were gone; so was the light through the crack in the door. She traveled the length of the hall, grabbed the handle, opened slowly.

Filing cabinets stood against each wall. The drawers were left open—contents pillaged. Not even an empty folder remained–no scrap of paper. She found the closest one, read the label. *R-Aspecticyn.* "God-damn."

There was another door across the room. The only other way in or out.

She opened it, and went through.

AND ABEL

A glass wall separated her from them.

They were hauling boxes of files into a truck. Dressed in red. Rifles hanging from their shoulders, getting in the way of their work. The glass was sound-proof. They moved in total silence, as if she were watching a movie with the sound turned down.

Observing them was a man, draped in crimson. A cape was clipped to his collar–hanging over his left shoulder. A peaked cap fit snugly over curled black hair.

She approached the glass.

Silence.

He turned, looked down at her with round, glass eyes. A gas mask.

The lights were either fizzled out or half-bright. They made him seem like a wraith. She looked him up and down; he was tall, but not abnormal. Something was clipped to his belt–some kind of baton. Black, and metal.

His neck tightened–speech. Two red silhouettes dropped their boxes–looked through the glass.

She checked over her shoulder, left and right–turned back to the window. The redhoods were moving faster. There were hundreds of files–tens of boxes. She continued down the hall. When she looked back, she saw the gas mask staring. A bend in the hall. The tension in her muscles dissipated. She remembered to breathe.

Clank!

She stopped dead. A door shutting–in the distance. She turned–peered around the bend at the window. There had been five redhoods in total. Now there were four. The remaining ones continued their work, while the gas mask observed them.

"Shit." She grabbed her pistol with both hands.

Pale blue fluorescents illuminated a crooked descent by stair. Yellow lines were painted on the tile floor, up onto the walls. Metal garage shutters stuck out against the paleness–labeled in black paint. They were all shut, except for one. Roxanne reached up, grabbed the shutter–pulled it down a little. *STORAGE: "R-ASPECTICYN".* Below were bold red letters. *HANDLE WITH CARE.* She let go and the door re-rolled itself. The tiling broadcast her footsteps. The stairs were worse. She passed by doors labeled with unknown names. *STORAGE: "FLUVELIN-74", STORAGE:*

"OXYPRETILYNE", STORAGE: "RUBELVA".

As the bend in the hall peeled back, it revealed an open door–and another through it, and another. A visual tunnel through rooms–like a mirror reflecting a reflection. He appeared through the farthest door–spit fire from his rifle.

Roxanne ducked behind the wall. Bullets snapped against the concrete–shattered the tiling. It stopped. She darted out, pistol first–fired a shot. It struck the crimson body armor and passed clean through. He hit a rolling table on the way down. His finger locked on the trigger, sprayed bullets in an arc.

One struck her shoulder. She gasped–ducked behind the wall again.

The clip emptied.

Silence.

She stepped out, examined the corpse through iron sights. Red cloth. Red mask. She stepped over, found the door he'd come through. Blood painted a streak down her sleeve.

Another hall. This time, the stairs snaked upward. There was a map on the wall with vague detail. A red dot indicated its position. Dark printed tunnels. A web, underneath the entire Cardinal property. She climbed the stairs, ignoring the shutters this time.

BANG!

Doors were flung open. He came through, saw her at the top of the stairway. Peaked cap. Gas mask. He unclipped the baton from his belt and it extended—wreathed in static shocks. "The doctor wants you dealt with, sweetheart. Come on over."

She aimed, fired.

He took the needle shot to the chest. It stuck in his breastplate. Two gloved fingers pried it out—flung it aside. "Little bee. Don't bother." A drawl. It almost slurred his speech.

She ran. Back down the stairs, over the body. Up the first stairway. Eventually, she came to the caged room, where the prisoners continued to moan.

A shout from behind: "Come on over, and we'll fix you up!"

The elevator lights washed over her. She tried the key, but it wouldn't turn. "Come on! Work, you piece of shit!" Harder. Harder. She wriggled it and twisted. *SNAP!* "Oh… fucking…" Pain shot through her arm.

He entered, saw her in the elevator.

The caged bodies began to wail. They shrunk away from the bars.

"Come on now, sweetheart. That's not the way."

A crescendo of sound. Moaning and wailing.

"Shut the fuck up!" He swung his baton, back and forth

against the cells. Lightning crawled up and down, snapping back and forth in between. The darkness was molested by flashes of light and sound–a strobe of heat.

Roxanne slipped out of the elevator. The flashing revealed a second door in the shadow, by the three gurneys– and the dolls. She sprinted for it, swung it open, then shut it tight.

Fast footsteps.

Crashing, then the door was kicked in. Smoke from the shocks leaked through the top of the frame into the room.

"I'm not gonna hurt you, sweetheart."

She sprinted backward, into something metal. A reclined medical chair–stained and torn.

"Come here."

His hand wrapped around her throat. She tried to speak, but her windpipe could only form a croak. She felt metal prods against her ribs. "N…o… F…u….c…" She screamed. Lightning shot out from the stick into her body–gnawed at every bone and burrowed through flesh. A cloud of odor came up with the smoke. Burning skin.

"How's that, sweetheart? Huh? You like that?"

Another shock. Another scream. She balled her fists and struck his head. The peaked cap fell off onto the tiles. She pulled at his curls, tried to pry the mask off his face, but it was tight.

"Leave that on. I'm ugly underneath." The baton came away for a moment–so he could grab her waist with his hand. He heaved twice, and flung her across the room, into a metal shelf. Clutter and plastic bottles rained down; she shielded her face. "Faster, or slower? Gotta tell me, sweetheart. I haven't got all day."

SNAP!

He struck a table. Sparks shot up and fizzled into black clouds.

She looked around, clutching her wounded shoulder. There were mannequin heads on the counters along the room's perimeter. Most were used to display things. Masks. But the masks were too life-like.

SNAP! SNAP!

They were all female. A tall mirror was bolted to the wall. In front sat an armchair. The cushions were stained.

SNAP! SNAP! SNAP! SNAP!

She looked up, saw the body lying in the reclined medical chair. Its head was skinned, hands degloved.

"Get up! I like it when you run, sweetheart!"

She crawled backward.

He followed, striking the shelves–knocking the heads onto the floor. One got in the way of his boot. The plaster crumpled like old paper; the mask became a wet, red stain. "Up! Up with ya!"

The pistol came up, fired another shot. It struck the gas mask–left cheek.

He groaned, reached up to pull the bloody needle from his face.

She ran.

Another door led to another hall. She flew down it, unsure where it led.

From behind came his voice. *"Run, little bee!"*

She popped out into the room with the glass wall. The redhoods had almost finished loading. The door she'd come through was metal–lockable. It slammed shut, and she sealed it with the swinging bar.

It rattled.

She waited.

Silence.

Now she did the same to the second door. The redhoods behind the glass were unaware. One jumped down through the loading door and vanished towards the front of the truck.

She wrinkled her nose. "Don't you…" The pistol's mouth kissed the glass. Her grip tightened. "Please work…" She turned her head–squinted.

Thwip! Thin webs were drawn through the glass pane. They emanated from the needle hole poked through. Now she could hear through to the other side.

"What the fuck?"

Bullets pierced the shattered pane. Roxanne dropped to her back—flat as possible.

The glass crumbled to pieces, unable to hold itself. As it fell, she saw a brief glimpse of red. A shot. It hit, and the redhood stumbled across the room unconsciously. Then the body collapsed in a heap.

Silence.

She listened. After a second, there were more footsteps, from around the front of the truck.

Thwip!

The driver's head struck the side of the truck, then the concrete.

She waited, then stood—dusted off her jumpsuit. Pain shot up and down her arm. Her boots clicked hollow on the truck bed. Around her were boxes, all labeled with the cardinal. Through the windshield, she could see the underground rampway that led somewhere—up, to the surface.

She felt around in her pocket. "Here it is, Sonny... We did it—I mean, one part."

A lighter.

"Maybe I'll burn the whole place down. Have mercy on those... people."

Flick! Flick! Flick!

Orange glow. She held it up to one of the boxes, then

another, and another. The cardboard caught and smoldered. She threw off a lid and scorched the papers. The inside of the truck was an oven now. She stepped out and waited–to make sure it burned.

PRO MEDICAL
PROGRESSUS

His face was projected on the wall. He sat at a desk–his office desk, with his hands folded on top.

"My name is doctor Osian Molina. I am Co-CEO and lead scientist here at Cardinal Medicine. I have been working in the fields of biology and neurosciences since I graduated high school. My father was a gifted scientist, and I loved to watch him work–take part in his experiments and listen to his hypotheses. He, I truly believe, would be proud of me today. Because today... I am going to reveal my discovery to the world.

"It is the understanding of most modern biologists and neuroscientists that the larger structures of our human brain are sufficiently uncovered and functionally understood. Yet they would admit that we, in fact, know very little about the processes these structures undertake in minutiae. There are approximately eighty-six billion neurons in our human brain. There is room for discovery here.

"During research conducted with my colleague Otis Lang, I stumbled upon a secret hidden from us. There is a shrunken cranial nerve, which I have dubbed "The Aurora". What its function is can not yet be explained, though it seems to respond to stimulation in the form of chemical prodding. Further experiments will be conducted. Soon enough, it will be understood why evolution tried to neuter this piece of us. The results, I am certain, will fascinate."

She stood at one of the four entrances to the main foyer. Smoke was in the air, drifting through the rays of sunlight. The tank was wedged into the wall from the outside–its metal arm halfway impregnated. The canister at the tip had emptied its gas, and the gas had long since filtered back outside. It sputtered.

Molina's projection had to pass through the smoke to reach the wall above the secretary's desk. Someone had clearly turned it on.

Death was strewn across the floor. The room smelled of viscera.

She crossed, heading for the reception desk as the projection looped itself.

A phone. She picked it up, pressed a button. After a second, she heard her voice from above, amplified. The intercom sputtered. She took a breath. "Your work is burned… Every page… and vial. I'm in the foyer… Come and talk to me."

Click...

The desk was flanked by two pillars. She went to one–hid behind in the shadow.

"...father was a gifted scientist, and I loved to watch him work..."

Time passed.

Then a door opened.

A wheelchair rolled into view. He was searching the room with his sunken eyes. His head gently shook in circles.

She didn't want to step out–to be observed by him.

But she did.

He smiled. "Roxanne. You... are a st-t-t-trong-headed woman."

"Why are you still here?"

He rolled in place–to face her. "I am w-w-w-w-within my c-castle. Outs-s-side I am easily dis-di-d-dispatched."

Silence.

"My r-r-redhoods will p-p-protect me." He tried to push his glasses up, shakily. "From the p-p-policemen."

Silence.

"Now you kno-kn-kno-know my secrets. Y-y-you went int-in-into my s-s-secret room."

"Who are they?"

"P-p-prostitute women. H-h-homeless m-m-men. P-p-p-people who ha-h-h-have no ident-t-t-tity." He paused. "Like y-y-you. No ident-t-t-tity."

Silence.

"I ha-h-h-have other d-d-drugs. C-c-contributions to the adv-v-v-vancement of m-m-medicine."

She wrinkled her nose. "If you did, you wouldn't have come to me when I called you."

His laugh was distorted–pushed through a collapsing tube. "Ev-v-verything I d-d-do is for m-m-m-medical advancement. Ev-v-verything. Y-y-y-you c-c-c-came to me w-with your c-c-cousin. All those y-y-years ago. You could hardly sp-p-peak English."

Silence.

"I c-c-could have made you one of my d-d-dolls. D-d-do you know that? B-b-but your cousin was s-s-so-s-so useful." He tried to straighten a crooked tie. "You are s-s-so like my s-s-sister. Same hair… s-s-same skin… s-same eyes… same body…"

She lifted the gun–kept her finger off the trigger. "Sonny didn't want me to risk myself trying to kill you. But I could… put a needle through your skull. All that evil would be gone in an instant. You would be a hunk of flesh. Useless and unremarkable."

"Y-y-you t-talk like a st-t-tudent philosopher. Like y-y-your c-cousin." A pause. "It would s-s-satisfy you… to k-k-kill me. Av-v-v-venge the whores and b-b-bums and idiots we used as g-g-guinea pigs. You w-w-w-were one of th-th-those i-idiots. Alb-b-bino rats in our m-m-maze. I w-w-wasted y-years of your l-l-life. S-s-stuck you in my p-p-p-prison. I never w-w-wanted you to c-c-come out. I w-w-wanted to see how l-l-long s-s-someone could stay inside. N-n-no aging. No disease. N-n-no desire to eat or sleep or c-c-copulate. A p-p-perfect stasis. The ext-t-tension of our m-m-mortal lives."

Silence.

"And y-y-you doomed us t-t-t-to d-death."

Her finger found the trigger. Her arm straightened.

BANG!

A muzzle flashed from the darkness. The bullet ripped through the back of the doctor's skull, erupting out his eye socket.

"No!" She turned, saw the redhood with the rifle. She aimed–fired. The needle struck and he went down.

Molina's corpse fell out of the wheelchair, no longer tremoring. He was dead.

Tears ran down her colorless cheeks. "Fuck!" She crouched down, head in her hands. Overhead, the projection ran uninterrupted.

"He, I truly believe, would be proud of me today. Because today... I am going to reveal my discovery to the

world."

She headed straight for his bed. The IV bag was still full of crimson liquid. She kneeled down, gripped the needle, and pulled it out. "Alright, Dewey, wake up." The bag came off its metal hanger. She took it to the attached bathroom, pulled a knife. It bit the plastic skin and spilled the drug–into the toilet. Once it was spent, she flushed, and set the bag on fire.

"Dewey!"

He wasn't moving.

"Hey, get up!" She felt his neck. There was nothing. She plucked off his glasses and opened both eyelids. "Fuck. No. What the fuck?" Her open palm felt around for a heartbeat. It didn't find one. She sat back on her haunches, rested her chin on the mattress.

There was a note.

And a packet of cookies.

Roxanne.

I hope you accomplish what you mean to do. I've been following you up until now, along with Sonny. We've been talking, and I've decided that I don't want to wake up. I'll be stuck in here with your cousin, but he's already made it beautiful for me. My wife is here. It's an illusion, maybe, but

I don't care. Sonny talks about you often. He makes you sound brave. You're young, and ready for the world. I'm old, and the world has given up on me. I understand now that my life has been awful–I've done awful things. It's best if I let it all go. Sonny's taking care of me.

Thank you, Roxanne.

She put the note down, lifted Dewey's albino-white hair. There was a wound. Gunshot, to the skull. Now she saw the pistol–*Ballester-Molina*. It was placed under his folded hands.

For a long time, she sat by the bedside in silence.

Then she heard tapping on the window.

She turned, searched the fogged glass. It was a cardinal. Their eyes met, then the bird fluttered off into the sky.

It started to rain.

ABOUT THE AUTHOR

Tony Del Degan was born on January 4, 2003 in the city of Calgary, Alberta. He is a Canadian author and visual artist who commonly writes in horror and science fiction genres. He is the lead editor and creator of Dug Up Magazine-a digital horror art publication, in which he seeks to platform upcoming artistic talent.

Visit tony.deldegan.ca to explore the Red Runnel universe.